First Edition

eBook ISBN: 978-0-9978791-6-2

Hardcover ISBN: 978-0-9978791-8-6

Copyright © 2023 Westin Lee

All rights reserved

Paranormal School 13

True Stories as Told by the Students of PS13

Westin Lee

To Cait and Kyle
the multimillion-dollar real estate kings

PS13 Campus Map

The Blue Cat
by Alexa

i missed the bus
and had to walk

i walked by a palm tree burned to a crisp
like a huge lit match
i cut through an apartment building
with hallways made of light
out front, was a girl in a ballerina costume
a man reading an old timey book
and a bench
on which they sat
the bus pulled up and out climbed a woman
who gave the man a nasty glare
grabbed her bicycle from the rack
and rode far, far away.

and then, to top things off
i walked the block
and out strolled a cat
as blue as the sky
as plain as day
she looked at me
as if to say, "why not?"
and i had to agree after the tree
and the hallway lights
and the girl in tights
the man with the book
who got that look.

so, i took the cat home
and wrote it this poem.

FALL SEMESTER

Alexa

[Alexa Garcia]

Okay. Right.

I got moved to a new school and this is my mandatory journal. They have a mandatory journal you have to write in here. That's new.

I am writing in the journal about being forced to write a journal.

Uh, I guess I should say a little bit about myself? My name is Alexa. I'm fifteen, and I live in Los Angeles. Like, actual Los Angeles The City with my grandma and my brother and my aunt and uncle. I like bad TV shows where people yell at each other in front of an audience or in a nice house or a place of business. I like frozen pizza (all varieties). My brother is fine, I guess. He and I get along mostly because grandma yells if we don't. No abuelita yells like ours can.

And I'm tall for a girl. I guess that's important to people. I don't see what the issue is.

And I have psychic powers. I guess? At least one? And supernatural powers are apparently common enough that there's a magnet school for students who have them? And there're at least twelve other schools like this because this one is number thirteen? And no one knows if you have the powers or not until you just blast them everywhere apparently? Maybe then someone could have told me about it before I ruined my life.

I'm assuming they read these, so I'll just leave it at that. Great first day! This website sucks, by the way. Is it from 1998?

[Ebit Nicole]

TRANSCRIPT OF MORNING ANNOUNCEMENTS FOR TUESDAY, AUGUST 14

Good morning PS13! This is Ebit Nicole and Don Chang.

The weather today is sunny and clear. Temperature will be ninety-two degrees.

This day in Paranormal School System history: Did you know the Paranormal School System has schools all over the world? From the frozen Siberian north to Perth, Australia, if you can hear the crackling howls of a naturally occurring Seero vein, you can expect there to be a Paranormal School there.

Lunch today is Turkey Blitz. Students without a permission slip will be able to get a sandwich pocket from the snack bar instead.

Are you using our website? PS13 provides every student with a login to our student intranet, where you can update your calendar, message faculty, and write in your mandatory student journal. You can even read other student journals! See what your classmates are up to! Is that plant man in the lobby of the 100 building made by Javier (who is your classmate)? Read to find out.

Spoiler—it is! He made the plant statue that slowly tries to grab you. Don't worry. It's safe.

That is all. Have a safe, productive day, Paranormal School!

Paranormal School 13

[Alexa Garcia]

Do you know Edendale High School? Over off Sunset Boulevard kinda near Echo Park Lake? I guess Edendale High School is an illusion of some kind, because once you're inside the fence, it changes and then you're at this school. The "real" school. Otherwise, the place looks like a normal high school. In fact, the buildings are even in the same spot, so when you go through the illusion field thing it looks exactly the same except inside there's more weird stuff.

What weird stuff, you ask, imaginary friend reading this journal?

Well... psychic powers are real, magic powers are real, werepeople (wolves, coyotes, mountain lions) are real, time travel is theoretically real (more on that later?), there is a cat person, there is a teacher that crawls on walls and an entire clique made up of human-sized animated wooden puppets. Their high fives sound like when a drummer clacks her sticks together. Clack!

Oh, and a boy flew out of a window (second story) and then someone yelled, and he got embarrassed or something and flew back inside.

How do people fly? Is that something they teach here?

I could go on forever. Let's do this. Every day, I will pick a Weird Thing of the Day, and write it down here.

Weird Thing of the Day: Uh, Edendale High School isn't real. Makes me wonder about the people I've met that said they go there. Are they students here?? Are they illusions??? Sometimes called "shades"????

[Alexa Garcia]

It turns out you have to have been born somewhere else to fly. Not like Arizona, I mean, like, I can't remember what the teacher said. Somewhere weird.

I should explain what it's actually like here.

The school is made up of lots of normal school buildings, a gym, and there's a track with a tall fence around it and a cafeteria. The

Alexa

buildings are all sort of spread around campus and the main classroom ones all are numbered, so 100, 200, and so on. Most of my classes are in the 200 building so I guess that's for sophomores. Sophomores, like me!

The weird thing is there's a 500 building, but as far as I know, we're out of here after twelfth grade. Maybe the problem students go there? All the windows are frosted so you can't see what's going on. Big enough to house a mechanic's garage and a wood shop, I bet. Then you go and work in the magic psychic flying equivalent of my friend's uncle's repair shop where they don't repair any cars.

I can walk from home, which is pretty nice. I've never been close enough to walk to a school before. I'm maybe three quarters of a mile away. Grandma used to yell at us about being out later around here because of unsavory types, but now she says the millennials have moved in and the neighborhood has changed a lot. I remember there being more laundromats, and now there are more coffee shops. And the laundromats that are left have new signs and are next to vegan noodle shops that are only open from noon to four p.m. She is skeptical of millennials, but I like the changes. It was hard to do stuff when my only options were old creepy bars that opened at sunrise.

Weird Thing of the Day: I am in a class called, uh, Mutable Realities. To prove a point the teacher made our textbooks fall upwards with an old timey TV remote. Like, they clicked a big button and all the books fell onto the ceiling as if they were falling onto the floor. And then the ceiling panels or whatever they are called also fell up, and we had to run out of the class while panels and books fell back down. I think our teacher got in trouble with the principal. They were talking quietly and then the teacher turned red. Not like a power—she just blushed like she was ashamed or mad.

[Alexa Garcia]

Amendment to that Weird Thing of the Day from yesterday, as the Weird Thing of the Day (Year?) for today: The teacher apologized to anyone who got beaned by a ceiling panel (*drop* ceiling panel, that's what they are called, haha). He said they were trying to make a point about "fate." Like, uh, I guess not everyone is bound by fate, but some people are? And to show that she broke out the remote and yeeted the books up again...

...except mine stayed.

My book just sat on my desk, and everyone looked at me. And then the teacher nodded and said, "Well, that's interesting, isn't it?" <u>And winked at me.</u>

Now that I think about it, I didn't say this earlier but when that principal or whatever, Dr. M? When he came over to my house and was meeting with me and Grandma and saying I was "special," he pointed to my birthmark (which is just a dot on my arm) and made some comment about how I "wasn't supposed to appear for a generation." Then he whispered that "Lurkett won't know what hit her," and he winked, like I was supposed to know what the flip that means.

Am I, like, supposed to fight an ancient evil? I'm betting that sort of thing happens pretty frequently here.

Hey, secret school people reading all these journals in a secret missile bunker! Am I supposed to fight an ancient evil?

Can you just tell me?

Maybe just use words instead of a wink?

What am I even saying?

[Mikey12]

Welcome to the school, Alexa. I'm new, too, so it's cool to read about new perspectives on this place from someone older and wiser (I am a freshman).

It's so weird here! Btw, be careful. There's a lot they aren't telling us. Did you hear about what happened to PS12? Are you really supposed to fight Lurkett? Oh, what powers do you have? Psychic, magic, dimensional, or miscellaneous? I'm a werewolf, so I'm one of the miscellaneous ones. Don't worry, zero confirmed kills. I haven't transformed in the wild since I was like ten. You should see the other were-students. They've really got problems.

Alexa

[Natalie Lavigne]

I think I may have bit off more than I can chew with joining Students for Safety again this year, but I'm so glad I get to do it. I am never bored. Doing five things is always better than doing three things.

[Alexa Garcia]

So. Um.

    I saw Bianca today when I was walking home. She didn't see me because the minute I saw her my cheeks got really hot, and my stomach did a twist, and I tried to hide. I know, it's stupid. All I could think about was the time we fought. Just the way her voice turned loud and mean and the look in her eyes…

    You know what? Let's do this. I will just refer to what happened as The Incident.

    Example use: All I could think about when I saw her was <u>The Incident</u>.

    And then she saw me and said hi, but she kept walking. So now all I can think about is <u>The Incident</u>.

    Why am I writing this in some public school journal? Who reads these?

[Mikey12]

Alexa, we're all on here! Hi. You know I'm writing to you, right?

    I said hi the other day and you didn't say anything. It's all cool if you don't want to talk, I just thought maybe you didn't hear.

[Alexa Garcia]

Hi, Mikey. Sorry. Yes, I can see your posts. I didn't even notice until today I saw the little red dot next to my name on the website. And I don't remember anyone coming to talk to me but maybe I just missed you. The hallways can get a little intense. Blue light flowers shot out of a locker today, like that old movie with the computers.

And I saw your question about powers. I'm psychic.

Did you say something about Lurkett? Who/what is Lurkett? Why am I supposed to fight her? What happened to PS12? Is that related? Are there other questions I should be asking?? Guessing yes???

Weird Thing of the Day: In Introduction to the Mind, they hooked us up to these machines that have big helmets on them, and cables run to a computer in another room. Then we took a standardized test. I asked what it was for, and the teacher just smiled. Anywhere else I would be like, "Well, this is just a state required test I guess," but here I'll just add it to the list of things I would never tell my abuelita.

[Mikey12]

Be careful about those machines, Alexa. I read online that scanner helmets aren't regulated, and no one knows how safe they are for psychics because they're so new. Someone really should be looking into this stuff!

Anyway, I'm super careful here. You've gotta be on your guard or you'll end up sucked into an energy vortex or swallowed by a monster and miss finals week and get held back.

That didn't happen to me (I am a freshman!), but I heard it happens a *lot*.

[Alexa Garcia]

Mikey, you are freaking me out. The teacher said the helmet was completely safe. Why would they have a class that hurts students?

Besides, it doesn't work for me. It's supposed to amplify your psychic thoughts so you can practice kinetics and reading and projecting to other psychics or whatever, but it didn't do anything at all.

Still waiting on an answer to what happened to PS12. And Lurkett. I'm assuming Lurkett is English?

Alexa

[Mikey12]

Oh, come on! Just because a teacher says something is safe does not make it safe. That's just what *they* want you to think.

Lurkett was/is an evil psychic that terrorized LA and then mysteriously vanished. <u>Supposedly</u> it was because she was defeated by a mysterious and powerful psychic from the future! But honestly that sounds a little far-fetched. A big earthquake happened the day she was defeated so I guess that completely normal-seeming thing was actually part of a supernatural battle against good and evil!

But hey, maybe that's just what *they* want you to think. ;)

[Alexa Garcia]

Okay, Mikey. Thanks.

I had a dream about my old school last night. When I woke up I really missed my friends. Bianca, Raza, Emi…

And then I was walking this morning and I ran into Bianca again, and she saw me again. Her car is broken so she has been walking to the bus. She was wondering where I went and why I wasn't at school. I didn't say that I was coming here because I know that's against the rules. So I said my grandma won a contest to get me into a private school and I didn't want to disappoint her. And actually, we talked for a little while, and after, she said it was good to see me and hugged me.

I know I can never make up for what I did, but I'm glad she can at least be nice to me for when we randomly run into each other. I said I had to go, which was true, and rushed here for first period.

And in first period, I made my first bubble around air! The teacher brought in a fog machine and fogged up the floor and we got down there and thought real hard and, sure enough, a little, glowing bubble locked in some wispy smoke. And then I gasped, and you're not supposed to do that because it's distracting, and it went away. But I did it!

You know what, mandatory journal? I'm gonna give it a shot. If Bianca can walk in her ridiculous heels a full mile to school, I think I can stick this out. Who knows? Maybe I can learn to control my powers and go back to normal school. And I still have no idea what this Lurkett thing is, but if I'm the chosen one, I'm the only one that can stop him/her/them/that. Okay, fine!

Today, fine, I'm your hero. Tomorrow… well, we will see how much time travel is involved in this thing.

Did I mention the time part? I don't remember.

[DOCTOR M]

Daily step count: 15,032

Spent the morning dealing with disciplinary actions:

1. Jasmine Bergdall got in a fight with Esmerelda. Esmerelda used an arcane swear word ("Fluzelt*ff") to transform an entire hallway in the 300 building into an ornate spiral staircase inspired by the aristocratic decor at Versaille. SFS is blocking it off now and will lead an astral search for the two students still missing. I have some questions as to the nature of that pair's "friendship." When I was a student at Santa Monica Underground, my friends and I did not try to trap each other in pocket realities.
2. JR Benton tricked two other students into running nude through the campus while projecting harmless but very exciting-looking psychic fireworks from their posteriors. They made it through the pool, then the 100 building, and partway through the cafeteria before a table of panicked freshmen used sensory barriers to keep light from reflecting off them, rendering them invisible. JR is sitting outside waiting for me, hearing about Grace's trip to Tahoe with her grandkids. He has developed a real rapport with her over the years.
3. The plant person in the 100 building is missing and Javier is panicking at a level I've not seen from a student in a while. Best guess is it just left. Slowly. But Javier has been

Alexa

screaming about it in his Clockworks class and it had to be dealt with.

In other news, I just checked, and I took the wrong information folder to the last new student home visit. The girl I visited was an Alexa, not an Alex. The folder read *G., Alexandra (Alex)* and I wanted *G., Alexandra (Alexa)*. Honest mistake and more evidence our filing system needs to be brought into the 21st century.

I may have strongly implied that she was chosen to defeat an omnipotent evil psychic entity from the 1990s.

I may have also pointed at a birthmark as if that was evidence that she was a chosen one.

She seemed excited at the idea, so I'll just leave it be. A new student needs motivation, and who's to say she won't find an ancient evil to defeat here? This last March was a veritable cornucopia of revenge ghosts.

Note to self: Check with Grace before taking folders out to meet with parents of prospective students.

[Natalie Lavigne]

I can bench press a bus! I can write a sonnet! I am Natalie and I can do anything. Hear me roar!

Not true, of course. The bus part I mean. Just looks like it. But turns out I can slip enough pressure underneath a corner of it to make it light enough for my compact frame to pick up. I only have to zip a micron and shift space in reality, like a wormhole bunching up space. Or like the latest theory says.

The sonnet is merely okay, but I can grow and learn and be stronger. Rarr.

[Phoebe Case]

Has anyone seen… I wanna say… it was a green, vinyl backpack? Next to the locker with the mouse castle inside. There fourth period, gone fifth.

Trying to keep it together.

The Question Society

[Ebit Nicole]

TRANSCRIPT OF MORNING ANNOUNCEMENTS FOR TUESDAY, SEPTEMBER 6

Good morning PS13! This is Ebit Nicole and Don Chang.
The weather today is sunny and clear. Temperature will be eighty degrees.
This day in Paranormal School System history: Did you know that in 1987, there was no September 6? Unexplained magnetic fields emanated from the northern tip of Alaska, from the last known location of famed psychic archaeologist and PS13 alumnus Dill Cross, causing the entirety of the planet to experience a fugue state lasting exactly twenty-four hours. The Paranormal School System assisted government and supernatural-aligned agencies over the course of 1987 and 1988 in creating a false day, with memories and records to match. Thanks to these substantial efforts, by the time the jumpin' 1990s rolled around, people had completely forgotten.
Today we also remember Dill Cross, from the PS13 class of 1980.

He once said, "In every seemingly normal ancient crypt is a world of mystery and chaos."

There is still no explanation as to what happened to our esteemed alum or to the day itself.

Lunch today is tater tots and gravy, my (Don's) favorite.

Do you have after school plans? PS13 has over forty official clubs, teams, and extracurricular activities you can join. You can make new friends, learn new skills and hobbies, and practice controlling your newly emerged abilities and curses. Here are some clubs looking for new members:

-Co-ed Intramural Rugby

-Library Restricted Zone Committee

-Geological Survey Watchers

-Chess Boyz

Let your homeroom teacher know if any of those sound interesting. Unfortunately, Students for Safety still has a lengthy waiting list and is not accepting new members at this time. Keep trying!

That is all. Have a safe, productive day, Paranormal School!

[Mikey12]

I walk the halls of this "official" charter school of the "Paranormal School System" and I just know something is up. Thankfully we just had the first meeting of the squad that's gonna uncover it all:

THE QUESTION SOCIETY
© 2017 Mikey12
(I came up with the IP in fourth grade)

That's right. Me and my friend Damien are starting an official club to keep track of all the mysterious mysteries that go down here. We're going to document it all, and when the gates of Truth Valhalla burst forth with all the accumulated truth we have exposed, you will be so buried in crazy facts about the conspiracies behind this place that you won't even know what to do.

I am chairman, so at the first meeting last night I made a motion that we would:

1. Expand our membership
2. Solve some mysteries
3. Make Damien reporter so he pays attention for once

All told, a good first meeting. There are five members now! Here's to five hundred more.

[Damien Cross]

Minutes from the first meeting of the PS13 'Question Society'
September 7

Attending:
Mikey Doze, chairman and founder
Damien Cross, reporter
Lyle Lemley, member
Phoebe Case, member
Sven Kovalik, member

- First motion, by Mikey: Damien is to be chastised for being five minutes late.
- Sustained by majority vote. Abstaining is Damien. Damien reports feeling very bad and promises he will be on time.
- Mikey asks for leads. Who has clues to investigate?
- Sven reports seeing an unusually green cloud, shaped like a wendigo (arctic deer monster) when staying after school last week.
- Lyle reports that this mysterious revolving door appears on campus between the hours of midnight and one a.m.
- Phoebe reports that Gertrude Baumgartner appeared to have a crush on JR Benton based on witnessed behavior in the B-Hall of the 300 building.

- Mikey displays phone video of an unidentified flying object. Damien notes it looks like a plastic bag caught in the wind. Mikey chooses the next official investigation item as the unidentified flying object.
- Mikey delegates investigative duties. Mikey will locate the source of the object. Damien will record minutes. Lyle and Phoebe will interview students to see who else has seen the object. Sven will use his special abilities to 'listen' to radio waves for government black site chatter.

MEETING END

[Lyle Lemley]

I just spent the afternoon interviewing students between periods. I even snuck into a couple of classes to ask around. In one of them—I don't know the name, but it was a junior or senior one—the students had a little action figure person in an aquarium on the teacher's desk at the front of the class. The action figure person was teaching from a tiny book. Surprisingly loud voice.

Phoebe and I walked to the 400 building after that. Phoebe was acting really weird. Does she... does she know she's at Paranormal School?

[Damien Cross]

Last night I had a dream I was lying in a hammock on the beach in Costa Rica. When I woke up, I was perfectly balanced on a beam suspended over a warehouse that was on fire.

I gotta be honest, the firemen explained three times what was happening but I don't really remember. They gave me a ride back to Silver Lake and now I'm just really tired. I don't know what's happening, but this luck stuff is getting outta control. Sometimes a guy has homework!

Oh, right. Mikey's club is today, too.

[Mikey12]

FYI, today's Question Society meeting will take place at the abandoned shack behind Old Man Rodriguez's house. The one with the peeling roof you can see from Sunset.

Damien, be on time. This isn't an orphanage.

[Damien Cross]

Mikey didn't even say during the meeting, but the UFO we investigated last week was just Oliver. I have Algebra with him, and he said it was him with his remarkably clear English! Then to prove it, he flew around the room and showed me his white puffy jacket that looks exactly like a plastic bag from a distance.

I wish Mikey wouldn't be so hardcore about his club. I just like hanging out in abandoned houses and following mysterious people. That's not super easy to find a club for as a minor. You sort of just have to go do it. There's no structure. I want structure!

[Mikey12]

Really productive meeting yesterday, even though Damien lost the minutes. I remember everything though. Ace at memorizing.

Look, I know I can be a little tough, but it's because what we're doing is important. The Question Society is here to make a difference.

Here're the mysteries we talked about:

1. Damien told us to investigate the new company moving into the old American Apparel factory, but no one thinks that is a mystery.

2. Doctor M's secretary, Grace, has a trinket on her desk that might be a cursed amulet. Theory: It must be cursed because why would she have some jewelry she doesn't wear? Grace loves jewelry.

3. Ms. Cartwright, who teaches Home Economics and English III, has been seen with young men that behave strangely around her and have hiking backpacks. It's likely she is a Campire, which is a vampire that loves camping in the woods.

The Question Society

We're obviously going after Ms. Cartwright. Exercise extreme caution, Questionites. Based on what I learned by reading about vampires and woodland horrors in the library, she's capable of anything. Especially around trees.

[Ms. Cartwright, Teacher]

I had a strange conversation with young Damien Cross today. I am not a woods vampire that lures camping men into my lair. I am a single woman who dates, and preferably dates hot young firemen. Speaking of, one of them is calling now.

I believe private teacher life things should be left out of school, but when said school is full of psychics and warlocks and witches and many other manners of supernaturally intuitive students, you just don't get to keep some things to yourself.

[Lyle Lemley]

Mikey is really mean to work for. Sven already quit, and after today I'm out, too. Solve your own mysteries, Mikey. Solve the mystery of why you're such a jerk.

Also, it's weird that Mikey is a werewolf but he doesn't care how he got that way. It's an actual mystery!

The Question Society

[Damien Cross]

Minutes from the third meeting of the PS13 'Question Society'
September 17

Attending:
Mikey Doze, chairman and founder and primary Questioneer
Damien Cross, reporter
Phoebe Case, member and associate Questioneer

- First motion by Mikey - discuss new mystery leads. For example, what is going on with "all the new students."
- Damien requests that the group discuss the loss of Sven and Lyle due to Mikey's behavior. Overruled by Mikey and Phoebe.
- Phoebe observes the Winterween Dance committee just opened up seats for new members.
- Mikey moves to table discussion of social gatherings indefinitely. Sustained by Damien.
- Phoebe observes that social gatherings are the most important thing we will all remember from high school.
- Mikey asks whether social gatherings are more important than cosmic nightmares that lurk in the Near Beyond.
- Mikey moves to select a next investigation topic.
- Phoebe votes to investigate the edgy-looking students who hang out under the track bleachers after school. Mikey votes to investigate reports that squirrels on campus have been genetically altered to be slightly smaller than normal squirrels.
- Damien abstains.

MEETING END

Paranormal School 13

[Phoebe Case]

Don't tell anyone, but I'm only posing as a student. I'm undercover, investigating Edendale High School. Something is up here, and Phoebe Case is on the case. Just like my name.

You may have seen me on TV. KTLA? Yes, that's me. Former TV news personality turned investigative reporter. Now you can find my work online at crackedcase.website. These electro journals are really useful. I don't even need to write anything down.

This place looks like a normal high school, but I think there are a couple of unusual things:

- One student is very pale. Like way more pale than normal pale people are.
- There are four classroom buildings for grades nine to twelve, each numbered 100 to 400, but then also a building called the 500, which I believe to mean that it is 500 feet to a side?
- There is one bus that the students refer to as the "moon side bus," and while I am pretty sure it is not from the moon. It is a strange bus, and no one has ever seen it arrive or leave. It merely is here or isn't.
- One of the teachers is transparent... or whatever it is when something is solid shadow you can't see any detail in, just an outline.
- There is an emergency exit door in the wood shop at night that leads to an endless underground parking garage. (Hey, who do I have to blackmail to get a pass into there, amirite?)
- No one has asked me to homecoming yet
- Homecoming is in December and is called "The Winter Solstice Dance" formally and "Winterween" in excited whispers in the girls' locker room.

The last one is tough because I am, I think, pretty together by teenage standards, and I am very popular at my gym. I would never agree to go out with a minor (big trouble awaits down that road), but I kind of wish someone would ask so I can say, "No, it is not meant to be. I am twenty-six. I am an undercover reporter investigating your school."

[Mikey12]

I'm calling an emergency meeting of the Society, tonight at 11:11 p.m., behind the 200 building.

[Mikey12]

Okay, well, no one showed up to the emergency meeting but me.

I guess there's no more Question Society. In its current form anyway. And honestly, I know it's my fault. I drove everyone too hard. This is… sorry, this was an unsanctioned student club. They were here to have fun and I wanted it to be all business. I drove away the intellectually curious. Drove them back to investigating the vast mysteries of the universe alone.

Phoebe, I guess, has moved on now that the crowd at the bleachers has accepted her. I saw her there today. She stood out because of her distinctly out-of-fashion jacket and hair. Like an alien abductee hiding amongst small town honky tonk riffraff.

I don't know what I'm going to do now. Surely, there's a place for ol' Mikey.

Perhaps my old haunts online. But will they welcome me back after I quit in such, um… a dramatic fashion?

Maybe I can get this werewolf thing going again.

[Damien Cross]

I guess the rumors about gateways that appear here on campus at night were true.

I was going to Mikey's emergency meeting to tell him I thought he was being a jerk and ask if he could just disband the stupid Question Society so we could go back to playing video games.

I <u>need</u> normalcy.

But once I was on campus I had to run and hide from this night security guard who chased me and I parkoured up over the 100 building and lost him by doing the leg split thing above a doorway.

That worked, but after, I got lost back behind the buildings, in one of those back alleys where trucks drop off cafeteria foodstuffs or whatever. It was very eerie, even by PS13 standards. A super high barbed wire fence towered on one side, and then there was just a long driveway with a bunch of flickering old lights and cracked pavement.

I got to the end with the truck dock—

Hey, how do they keep the truck straight when they have to reverse for that long?

Anyway, to the left was a stairway down the hill to the teacher parking lot. But set into the stairs was this round mirrored door. It was like a heblit hole, but obviously those are vertical and this one was slanted into the stairs.

I know my uncle Dill vanished investigating strange things, but I can't *not* investigate mysterious doors. And it did open, and, well, you see a lot of weird stuff at a school like this, but this one is wild even by that standard.

[Cole Abrams]

They keep asking me to play rugby, but I won't do it. I've got five little sisters (quintuplets), and I worry enough as it is that I'll pick one up and accidentally throw her through the ceiling. They're small and always moving. It's a growing concern at home.

    Also, I'm busy.

    But it's mostly the fear of launching someone.

[Bobby Flay]

We just did block day for the play on Saturday and it's going to be so good. Nancy, you're a genius.

    Everyone, put the premiere in your calendars! Or it's curtains for you!

    Just a li'l theatre joke.

[Proto the Robot]

Gomez's new satchel is acceptable. Faux grain leather. Two pockets.

[GOMEZ]

Thanks! I got it to keep my papers crisp.

[Proto the Robot]

Nouto's brooch is acceptable. Bronze, handmade, possible mystical properties. A gift.

[Nouto Hashimoto]

Thanks, Proto. Your face is acceptable! The brooch was a gift from Okaa-san during our summer in Perth!

[Proto the Robot]

I do not require travel.

[Nouto Hashimoto]

Okay, well, I didn't ask.

[Proto the Robot]

Alexa's shoes are unacceptable. Many holes, two on the right sole. Converse High Tops purchased two years ago.

[Alexa Garcia]

I have other shoes. I just like these ones. They're comfortable.

    Is anyone going to explain why Proto acts like a robot, but he is just a little guy? All he ever does is make observations, and at a level of detail that's uncomfortable. Did you see the one about the thread count in Marcus' anime shirt?

    Is he secretly really a robot? At this point I wouldn't be surprised.

[Proto the Robot]

Ms. Cartwright's desk is acceptable. Six pictures in frames on it. Four of her Cairn Terrier Muscles, one of her daughter, Casey, one of her current boyfriend Ben.

Ben is a fireman.

[Juan Addams]

Whoa. I thought that guy was her son.

[Cole Abrams]

There was a fight in the courtyard near the flagpole today. Sometimes people need to blow off steam, but they were starting to use powers and that's a serious issue. I was the first SFS (Students for Safety) member on the scene. And lucky, too, because psychic barriers are good at nullifying magic, and this was a couple of wizard punks.

So, I've got them each in their own barriers and they're trying to magic their way out, but the spells just keep zapping against the barriers and making little ripples, bouncing around inside and frying their robes and giving them little shocks. I may not be much of a psychic when it comes to reading minds and stuff, but I wouldn't want to get into a physical altercation with me.

Puffs up chest

A House With No Windows and No Doors

[Vert Merpson]

This is a joke. It has to be a joke

A teacher assigned me to Gomez again for a class project.

I specifically asked not to be assigned to Gomez because the last time he was a nightmare to work with. Just a nightmare. I didn't write about it here because, well, it wasn't the weirdest stuff happening.

The project is a report on Echo Park, the normal version, with all the "normie" history, including the fabricated history of Edendale High School. And then that's threaded into the real, secret history.

Well, sure enough, Gomez sits down and is all smiles and even has a pen ready to go from nowhere (an otherspace outside our reality?) when mine crabs out, and his slicked-back dark hair caught the light perfectly and he smiled and complemented me on my vintage polo shirt and suggested going to Bandido Cafe after school one day to work on everything. But I'm not fooled.

I am not fooled Gomez!

A House With No Windows and No Doors

[Vert Merpson]

I feel bad.

Gomez approached me after class today and asked what was wrong with the project, if there was a reason I was avoiding talking to him. He just shrugged and looked up at me with eyes filled with earnest concern and I couldn't bear it. I told him I would meet with him at the coffee place, and he looked so, so, so relieved.

Ugh. Here we go. Maybe I just imagined things?

[Vert Merpson]

I am definitely not imagining things.

There's this coffee place on Sunset, and there's all this traffic when I walk in. Gomez jumps up and waves. He is super excited and asks me how basketball practice was, I said it was none-a-ya business (it was bad), and we sit down and the books crack open. We start going over the first part about the Sunset Junction Rift and how that complicated construction of the 101 freeway. Things are going great, and I have to admit, outside of whatever it is Gomez is doing or causing or bringing with him, he has the soul of a gentleman fifty years his senior.

And then I noticed that red truck driving by again. In fact, the only cars passing by outside weren't cars at all. They were old red trucks? A whole street of red trucks. Gomez's back was to the street, so I asked him if he saw it. That kid turned around, and stared at that street of red trucks, and just said, "Huh."

Huh like, "Oh, nuts, I'm out of butter," or "Huh, the Moonside bus is here again, and I didn't even see it arrive."

But then a bunch of expensive normal cars whooshed by when the light turned green, so I just shrugged it off. I am thinking about it again right now, and I'm starting to get worried.

[Vert Merpson]

Eric asked me why I was freaking out so much about Gomez, so let's all put our memory caps on and zoom back to the olden times of last school year. Fall semester.

Gomez and I were, yes, in Near History, and he is the same little, short kid that I tower over and he's still just disarmingly nice. At first I was like, "Does this kid *like* me like me or what?"

But no, we found out really fast when there was a notes incident in class that this was not the case. I was passing a note asking that question and JR Benton, being a jerk as usual, projected the contents of the note onto the ceiling ("Do you think Gomez likes me? He's disarmingly nice all the time") with such a powerful force of will that the drop ceiling panels faded slightly. The note is now forever imprinted into the ceiling. Everyone was laughing and I was super mad. Madder than I think I've ever been.

But Gomez just shrugged and said, "Of course I like them. I like everybody."

That was what made me initially think maybe we should be partners for the last project. It was a short presentation in class about the Graduation Incident at PS6—the one we all have to learn about because of how awful it was so it will never happen at any other Paranormal School, especially not one in a major population center like PS13 is in (or PS6 is).

So, we start working on this project on a Monday (it was an in-class-only project, no homework), and things are going fine, I guess. Except that I keep seeing stuff change in the room. No big deal. This is PS13, right?

Well, Tuesday happens and then that faded imprint on the ceiling reads something new. No, really, it turned into different wording. ("*DOES* Gomez like me? He's so nice all the time.") And no one would believe me. It was like they all thought nothing had changed.

By Wednesday there was a feral blue cat (like *BLUE* blue) that no one else could see that followed me everywhere, and when we gave the presentation on Thursday, none of my classmates had eyes. Just blank fleshy dents on either side of their noses.

I make it sound like this was not a problem, but it was a very, very big problem, and everyone was acting so normally that I didn't know how to react. So, I just stood there and they said, "Thanks for the report," and I went and hid in one of the bathrooms, which thank goodness, are the only reliably normal part of this crazy school. When I came back to class, everyone's eyes were back in their heads and Gomez had returned to his seat safely across class.

Eric is saying that this is *correlational* and that the story doesn't prove that Gomez is causing all the weird stuff. Now he's talking about a time he could change everyone's hair color at once by setting the time on his watch. You're not helping, Eric.

[Vert Merpson]

Something is really, really wrong in my neighborhood. I think I'm going to tell a teacher.

As you may know, stranger journal, I live nearby.

Echo Park has all these hilly neighborhoods all full of old bungalow houses that were built in the 1920s. I think they're kind of cool, with their columns and cute windows and green and yellow sides and their little porches. Some are way up high on steep hills, so you have to walk up two flights of stairs just to get to your front door. And the car driveways are just two concrete strips up an incline with a little old-timey car up top. It's a whole vibe to walk to school through the neighborhood.

Except, well, today I looked up at a random house and something was wrong with it. It doesn't even make sense, but well, there were no windows or doors on the house anymore. It was just blank walls with peeling paint in those bright colors, an old-timey car parked way up that narrow little driveway.

A house with no windows and doors—how does that even work? I know everyone is talking about these mystery doors on campus, but those are only supposed to appear at night. This was just an hour ago.

And this is an absence of doors, not the appearance of doors where there shouldn't be any.

...

I'm going to find Gomez and punch him right in his warm, beaming smile.

[GOMEZ]

It's the curse again.

[Vert Merpson]

I wasn't able to get home today.

School let out same as always, and I walked right out past the buses, same as always, and same as always, the Moonside bus left when I was looking the other way, off to parts wherever, and just like always, Maria didn't want to walk or acknowledge me, even though we walk the exact same way home.

Except... well, we rounded the corner that shoulda gone to Sunset where I cross into my neighborhood, but there was no way out. Just a wall of... houses? That's the only way to describe it. A wall like two or three houses tall made of bungalow walls, with white fixtures and little porches, with no windows and no doors.

I tried walking up the hill to see if I couldn't just go another way, but when I hit the top and looked down, I saw the "wall" extended all the way around to this side, too. I started to panic. My parents would be worried. I had chores! I sat down and tried to think of what Students for Safety taught in special assemblies for situations like these and came up a big, honking blank.

I'm just a junior! A year ago, I was worrying about how I was going to get home from the mall and whether James Golly would look too short next to me if I asked him to the Winterween dance.

Incidentally, those were also solid reasons why I knew I was too young to die. I had to figure this out.

Then I realized... this was a neighborhood full of people, right?

A House With No Windows and No Doors

Maybe Maria was nearby. I ran back down the hill and when I looked down the street, I actually saw her, walking towards the bungalow wall. I called out to her.

"HEY!"

She stopped and looked.

Then she pointed at her watch—<u>sorry I don't have time for you</u>—and walked through the wall.

I ran to where she had gone through and pressed my hands against it. It was definitely a wall. Logic dictated I should try some other spots, but I could see where this was going. I ended up heading back to school and now I'm sitting in the library dreading when Ms. Cartwright decides it's time to kick me out. I figured this would be a good journal entry, right? In case I starve to death in the neighborhood?

[Vert Merpson]

No one is responding right to this whole thing. I know what you're typing. *Vert! Why didn't you talk to a teacher?*

Well, I <u>did</u> thank you, and Ms. Cartwright and Mr. Jarvo and Ms. Smith and even Grace the Secretary all basically just smiled and nodded when I said I needed help.

What the flip! What am I supposed to do?

Think Vert. Think.

...

I just remembered something. Gomez and I worked on the project earlier today and I totally laid into him about the neighborhood and all the stuff that's happened. I mean I really wiped the smile off his little mustachioed face, and he turned super red. He didn't even say anything. He just left, and everyone was staring at us. I had sorta forgotten about it because I guess it was pretty mean. But he's the one doing all this stuff, right? He's the only person that seems to actually react when I saw what's going on.

Is this because I'm a bad project partner? Am I supposed to learn a weird ghost lesson or something?

No, surely not. But then again, some directed lessons are cruel and irrational.

Anyway, when Ms. Cartwright said it was time for people to leave, I ducked behind the shelves and hid when she checked the library. I don't wanna be trapped outside. It's cold! I'll just figure something out. Maybe I can apologize to Gomez, and all this is gonna go away and I can go home and I'll learn a lesson in forgiveness or something.

[GOMEZ]

This is so embarrassing.

How do you tell someone you got a curse because once upon a time, you did a math project with a witch, and you made her do all the work?

I am impressed Vert keeps working on the report because the curse is supposed to scare people so they will never work with me again. It preys on my intense love of others by making them suffer for my laziness.

There is no way to explain this. Curse rules. Alas.

I have not been a lazy partner in two years. I am reformed. I wish Alyssa would take the curse away, but she transferred to PS12 right before it disappeared and all my extensive research in the Restricted Wing of the library informs me there is no way to diffuse it (yet). Now Vert is really upset, and they think a tearful apology about yelling at me will help.

It won't. Only one thing will end this, and I can't tell them what.

[Vert Merpson]

I woke up in the aural meditation room to find that the bungalow wall was now at the windows to the school.

I knew what I had to do. I ran to the entryway by the office and sure enough Gomez was walking into the school exactly on his weird clockwork schedule. I went with the best, most public, cry-apology about how I was a bad partner and stuff, and Gomez sat there like he had gotten this one before. I thought maybe I had better amp it up, but then he stopped me because the ceiling had split open above us and porch columns had begun to snake into the hallway.

He could see it, too! Actually, everyone could.

It was a mess. Before, only I could see the bungalow wall. But whatever this stuff was was visible to everyone. Students were running and screaming, and columns were busting open lockers and making their way into classrooms. SFS teams tried to make a barrier perimeter but that didn't work. Then they teamed up with the faculty sponsors to make a bigger, more professional barrier and tried shooting lightning at the bungalows. And that didn't work, and we all ended up in the gym like it was a student assembly except people were shooting psychic beams into the doorways to keep vinyl siding and cute little old-timey garages from getting inside.

But Gomez seemed to know what was going on. He pulled a paper out of his bag. It was his half of the report! He asked if I had mine, and of course, seeing as how I was trapped here overnight, I had just written the thing out. He paper clipped them together and we dodged a rogue wicker chair deck set monster and ran for class. I slammed that report down on Ms. Brown's desk.

And that did the trick, I guess, because when we looked out in the hall, everyone was spooked but there were no house parts tearing up the school. It was like it hadn't happened. Students and faculty just kinda shrugged, picked up bags and papers, and went to class.

SFS got us and I had to give a big report that went into a red folder, and Gomez finally had to tell them about his curse. He now has a special class he goes to, I guess. The moral of the story was, um, always do your part of a group project.

Or maybe there is no lesson, and this is just a Thursday.

[Vert Merpson]

I just got home and was really expecting to get it for not coming home last night. But I guess the school administration's note is a little more than just paper and ink, because there was talk of a "special lock-in project" for class. Since it's a magnet school, the parents think I'm just learning to be a fashion designer, so they were like "Did you make some belts?"

On the walk home, I cruised past that first house up on the hill, the one I noticed first that had no windows and no doors. And well, it still had no windows, no doors, and a super steep driveway.

I think I should tell an adult about that.

[Annabelle Yes]

It's me, Annabelle. I'm president of the student council and also probable salutatorian. I would be valedictorian at any normal school, but this is a magnet school, and you just have to deal with the talent pool here. I try to impart this kind of patient understanding to the Type-A students I mentor. Natalie, I'm looking at you. Be mentored.

Word has gotten out that I'm one of just a few students who can make interdimensional portals, and I got about fifty messages on here asking for little favors.

"Warp me to Nashville so I can hang out with my cousin."

"Have a party happen in Doctor M's office."

"Help me get my earbuds out from the bottom of that drain grate."

No way! I don't use that stuff for fun. And neither should you, if you ask me. It's not a toy. I mean, I got the glow during a solar eclipse. That's not even how Vector powers are supposed to work. What if the next eclipse (lunar or solar!) just sucks it right back up? Back to Hollywood High for me. Maybe with a memory wipe.

I've heard it a thousand times. "Just make a portal to behind my head so I can see how I look from the back." No one likes what they see. It sucks the fun out of an evening.

[Alexa Garcia]

I do not get bars. You go there and… what? Drink gross alcohol in the dark? Abuelita says it's what idiots do. One time my little brother came home with some bottle he and his friends got ahold of and there was a cataclysmic discussion.

So, there's this bar on the way to the Bandido Cafe. One of the ones with dark inside and concrete floor and the patterns on the ceiling and a TV playing some sports thing that is not women's soccer.

They're always just opening when I go by, and it's weird but I love the smell. It doesn't smell like booze, like my uncle's cookouts. It's this fresh smell, like I'm walking by the open, drying door of a massive dishwasher that has just power-cleaned its insides. Like inside are a bunch of freshly machine-cleaned plates and glasses and I need to hurry up and put them in the cabinet because my brother didn't bother to do his chores.

Then there's a stop to ruminate in the presence of the airbrushed flapper girl with cool short hair on the side of the tattoo shop, and I'm in the cafe with all the other PS13 students. I get a long black, which is a gross Australian coffee that will keep me up well past midnight.

What a life.

[Mikey12]

Hey I'm not dead, FYI. And neither is anyone else because of me! Because I am a werewolf with zero confirmed kills!

That's because I've been using my newly acquired free time to work on myself. And specifically, my werewolf side.

I bet you have a ton of questions, so I typed up a little questionnaire that covers the ones I think I'll get the most.

Qs n As:

You're a werewolf?

Heck yeah, I am! How did you not know that? I guess I don't ever talk about it. I'm not embarrassed or anything I just don't want the extra attention, y'know?

How did you become a werewolf?

Great question, journal. I don't remember. It happened when I was real young. My mom says it was because she told me not to wander off too far and then I didn't listen because nobody tells Mikey Doze what to do!

She also said once that it happened because I was sticking a fork into an electrical socket even though she told me not to.

I have a series of scars that are chomp-shaped also. From my shoulder down to my belly button! Which one do you think it is? Let me know in the comments.

Can you "turn wolf" on command?

What a private question! JK.

That's what I'm working on! Normally, you gotta wolf out when the moon's out, but I know mysteries and adventures could really use a werewolf on command. I've tried a bunch of stuff but so far the only time I wolf is when it's a moon. And then I'm in the basement in the special room my dad built. There's a thicc tree trunk in there I can go ham on. You know I do!

Hey, upperclassmen! Help a were-boy out! Let's experiment, uh, with teaching me to control me powers. Just leave me a message.

What's next for investigating conspiracies at PS13?

Hang on someone is yelling outside. Be back.

Cole and Nat

[Natalie Lavigne]

Guten Tag everyone. Just a reminder that while we deal with the Nights of the Round Table [sic], SFS needs everyone to steer clear of the southeast corner of campus. Basically the corner of the track and that pair of benches where the cool edgy students usually sit. We're pretty sure the trouble with the Nights of the Round Table [again, sic] is over, but every couple of weeks reality alarms at SFS HQ trip and all our phones blow up with warning texts. You've probably heard the disembodied voice yelling, "FOR NIGHTTINGHAM!" over and over for no reason? Yeah, steer clear if you do.

If you have any questions, just talk to anyone at the Students For Safety HQ in the 400 building over next to the Paranormal Ledger room.

Okay, thanks.

[Aiden Chang]

Did anyone see that thing over at the track today? It was wild. The corner of the track just blipped the flip up and there was this portal, and everything was all distorted and I could see <u>another PS13</u> on the other side, like a mirror! But then there were lots of students trying to come through and they were all grinning but also running at top speed. Which if you've never seen someone do that, it looks very wrong.

I was really scared when I saw myself come through. I looked different because I had long hair that I cut short before I went to high school. Big disturbing grin as I hop through and where "I" stepped, the grass and stuff on the field turned black. It was really scary.

But then some teachers came and the SFS students showed up (you can tell who they are because they have those special green bracelets with the button on them). They made an energy barrier around the portal together and then the tall Black guy and the tiny pale girl with the red spiky hair ran in and read from a book. And all the alternate universe students just sort of turned around (still grinning!) and went back in their portal. The last one even turned around and closed it from their side, like they were zipping up a dress.

It was seriously cool! And the grass on the field is still burned in these concentric radiating circles out of where the portal was. It's crunchy when you walk on it.

[Camel Riboy]

I used to think Student Safety or whatever was super lame with their communicator wrist bands and how they always stop you from starting mind fires, but after Cole and Natalie stopped that stack of books that was moving like a person, I think they're pretty cool.

Or maybe it's just those two? They're cute together, right?

[Natalie Lavigne]

Hola! Annabelle was asking about the paper I wrote about being in Students For Safety (SFS). So:

"A Day"
    By Natalia E. Lavigne

We sail over the table. One big jump for me, more of a large step for Cole. The group of Vector cultists scatters in every direction, but the 4-D Hypercube at their center remains, folding in on itself impossibly. This close, I can feel its pull, the urge to walk into the fourth dimension like the clarion call of the manga section of a bookstore. It would disintegrate us all if it could. Nothing makes a Hypercube rage like the presence of 3-D entities.

The pull is almost too much. The urge to go home, even though I know it isn't really home. Not anymore.

I feel Cole's hand on my arm, bringing me back. I steady myself next to him and we unfold the incantation notes we copied. I read first. The line is hard to pronounce but I get close enough that it starts to work. Cole reads his part, and the first stage is complete. The cube seems to shiver and shrink just slightly. It's hard to tell with all the corners and edges flowing into and out of it. I zip up to the upper level of the library. The little electrical arc from hopping dimensions plinks off of the wooden banister with dull taps I can feel all over. The hair on my arms stands on end.

At this point, at the most important point, my mind begins to wander. I find myself weaving through my day—the homework that's due, the college applications and summer internships on my little vintage desk I painted sky blue, the permission slip I forgot to have signed for the expedition into the Memorial Restricted Zone in Griffith Park.

Cole and Nat

I think of home, of Dad and Mom. They'll be there tonight. They'll have their questions.

And I think of Cole, who told me half a joke earlier and then sauntered off, leaving me hanging. He does that. The guy is so unfazed by anything. Even a conversation can be left half-finished in his world. I bet he doesn't even sweat at surprise tests in Torreflot's Advanced Decahedron Navigation class.

So, what <u>is</u> a school of fish with water control abilities called? Will I ever find out?

My distraction <u>should</u> put me in danger. The incantation cracks but holds. Cole's circled back around the 4-D Hypercube and discovered that the folding is slightly different on that side. He fires another incantation. Vivaldi's <u>L'Estate</u> blares perfect music math from the sheet music he holds up. Hypercubes *hate* Vivaldi.

The Hypercube collapses until it is a normal 3-D cube, then a 2-D square, and then it is a point, and then it is just a feeling of mild irritation that fades.

We help clean up with other SFS members and students. No one is seriously hurt but there was a cut arm. I get them off to the nurse. Zip! With the disappearance of PS12 this spring, the annual curse season, and an unusually high rate of dark prophecies maturing, Students For Safety is so important. Being in SFS is exciting and dangerous, but knowing I have a partner I can count on makes it all a little easier.

Cole and Nat

[Cole Abrams]

Nat,

Did you read the Normal's Family in the Ledger the other day? I know you don't normally read comics, but I thought it was funny and it made me think of the SFS video they made at PS6 about the time with the sinkhole that worked like a hurricane.

Ask me about it later. I have to go to rugby practice.

[Natalie Lavigne]

Sir,

I did read it because you recommended the one last week about Norma's uncle and now I like the comic. I still haven't met Chuck Quimby but maybe she will show her face if you ask nicely? We juniors live in a different world, where the comic artists are not.

And you have not said anything about Letters to Now. Have you abandoned me? I remember some bold statements made about how that book would be read in a day.

[DOCTOR M]

Daily step count: 15,035

A big hat off to SFS and star super squad Cole and Natalie for their prompt disabling of the arcane device placed in the Spellcraft practice arena.

Initial results from testing the device hint at a jack-in-the-box type made using Stellar Rembrandt Assemblies. This sort of highly dangerous magic could have caused a Sea of Dirac to swallow the entire 400 building, the practice range, and probably the teacher parking lot. Paranormal School System mathematicians have theorized that this sort of irresponsible nonsense may have been the cause of PS12 vanishing last year.

When I find out who placed it (probably JR Benton) there will be a disciplinary action so grand and horrifying that no one will ever break the rules ever again.

Thanks, Cole and Nat. You have pulled us back from the brink.

[Cole Abrams]

Nat,

I like writing back and forth on here. I mean, we see each other all the time, but this is good stuff. I didn't used to like writing in my mandatory journal but writing to you makes it easy.

[Natalie Lavigne]

Thanks, you.

I do think we make a good team. Mostly I just like the way troublemakers react when they see you towering over them, ready to put them in an impervious psychic barrier. And... me, also! Somewhere nearby, also looking very tough, but a bit smaller.

[Synthea Fluffson]

Oh, man, did y'all see Natalie and Cole in the 300 building hall today? Their outfits matched and they look SO. CUTE. TOGETHER. How long have they been dating?

[Cole Abrams]

Um, I think there's some confusion. Nat and I aren't dating. We are just friends. Just friends. And SFS partners.

[Natalie Lavigne]

Haha. My tall, broad friend, I think you doth protest too much. Let them know the truth! We have torrid romantic encounters under their noses, and all over the fanciest, rose-petal-strewn parts of Los Angeles.

Cole and Nat

Why lead them on? Tell them about the infamous summertime Walk Down Sunset, and the kiss at the end where I had to do a 24" vertical jump so our faces could interact. Tell them about the poetry read under the Solstice Mindstorm, where you told me I was the reason you run so fast and save the day so much.

[Cole Abrams]

Um, so it's safe for everyone to look at the 500 building again. The super bright silver lining around the bathroom doors has been dulled and the mysterious cloud entity that placed it has been driven away. More info in the report, but since the investigation is ongoing, I—we—can't say too much more.

Thank you.

Paranormal School 13

[Cole Abrams] [personal log]

Okay, official post is up but there's more to say. This one was really nuts. My powers didn't work quite right.

I'm psychic, yes, so I fall into that corner of the PS13 logo, but I've never quite been able to do much psychic reading. Psychics can generally do the same stuff with practice. Read minds, talk to each other without words, and move some stuff around. Reading minds is the hardest skill, but the truth is I'm lousy at a lot of the other ones, too.

What I have is this super super strong ability to make barriers. They didn't even know what to call them at first when all these disciplines were getting researched and documented in the 20th century. It's really just strong psychic energy in a flat kind of wafer thing. And I've gotten pretty good at those barriers. They're strong enough to block energy blasts and spells. They can protect me from a fall or pick someone up and hold them. Some of the smaller ones have that reverberating oomph you want from a good kick drum.

But whatever that silver sheen on the bathroom door frames was went right through it, and I've never felt so vulnerable. It was the first time in a long time I ever felt scared in SFS. It didn't hurt. It was just like getting intense sunshine diffused through water vapor.

When I got home, I felt really weird and rattled. Malia started climbing up to my shoulders and her little kid hands felt too warm and... I don't know. I think I might see the nurse tomorrow. Maybe it's nothing.

Cole and Nat

[Alexa Garcia]

Hmm. I feel like I shouldn't comment on this, but I just…

What's up with all the upperclassmen bugging Cole and Nat? What if they don't want to be a couple? Look, we're all young and feelings are confusing and just because something looks like a good idea doesn't mean it is. That's why I don't get the couples pawing at each other all over school. The ones especially that have been together for years. You started dating in seventh grade and you're still going? Really? You don't think maybe, just maybe, you don't know what you're doing?

Look if you really like someone, that's great. But let's be honest here. None of this is gonna last, so why don't you let them be friends?

[Natalie Lavigne]

Ah, you don't say a word to me and now this businesslike response. Did I cross a line, sir?

[Cole Abrams]

No, no, you're right! We should tell them the truth about our totally real and secret romance.

Okay, so Nat and I are partners half the time and the rest of the time we are adorable snugglebugs. My favorite part about Nat is that she dyes her hair every week regardless of whether it has faded or not. When I first met her, I actually thought that stop sign red was her natural hair color.

I also really like how she messes up her hair to appear bigger and tougher, even though she doesn't need that help to be intimidating. Never has someone that is maybe 5'1" been so terrifying.

Also, she has never heard this but the reason I couldn't talk on the first day of the year was not shyness. It was because she wore that leopard print outfit and it seriously messed me up.

Wait, that is actually shyness, right? Is shock a form of shyness? I'm going with yes.

Anyway, she is tiny and she makes me laugh on the inside, and I am glad our torrid romance is now public knowledge so all the hand holding and stuff doesn't need to be in secret anymore.

[Phoebe Case]

I knew ittttt.

Lots of couples have style but so few know how to reaaaally do just wall-to-wall-how-are-they-even-a-thing-this-is-too-good cute. And they save us regularly from our own naiveté. And also from impossible math monsters. Which I assume are metaphors for the everyday trials of high school.

When is the wedding you guys?

…

I hope one day I find my Cole equivalent (or Nat equivalent?). Just not here because you all are so young! I hope my innocent delight doesn't blow my cover.

Cole and Nat

[Natalie Lavigne] [secret diary]

Dearest Millie,

Oh my.

A couple of days ago the undercover reporter lady made some crack about how Cole and I were a cute couple, and I went along with it. I made a semi detailed joke response, with specifics, just like Ms. Cartwright taught me. Specifics are at the core of good comedy.

But the response I got from Cole implies he might be a little bit more... not joking. Is he joking? I mean, obviously we are not dating and haven't ever done anything but contain crises and share interesting books and comics.

But those examples are so specific in his response. He remembers what I was wearing the first day of the year. And I struck him silent with that getup*? He knows I dye my hair and that I muss it up to look big? He thinks I'm terrifying??

It made me feel... well, charmed I guess. Flattered. I didn't expect it. Would you be, Millie? He's noticed little things and I felt real affection. Why doesn't he say this stuff out loud? He is not good at words.

Ugh I don't know what to do. I don't even know if he was serious. Maybe I have just been one-upped at my own game.

*Said getup was indeed supposed to strike silence into someone, but that was for one Eric Vidali, who is still in so much trouble for events covered in this journal from pages 66-103. He has a long way to go to meet expectations, but we'll get him there.

[Ebit Nicole]

TRANSCRIPT OF MORNING ANNOUNCEMENTS FOR THURSDAY, SEPTEMBER 29

Good morning PS13! This is Don Chang. Ebit Nicole is absent today, recovering after the field trip to Atwater Village.

Teachers assure us Atwater Village is a completely normal place and that their many cute cafes and restaurants are completely safe.

The weather today is sunny and clear. Temperature will be seventy-one degrees.

This day in Paranormal School System history: The end of September is greeted with apprehension by all PS13 faculty and students. Starting October 1st, a month of imminent danger awaits us all. Since the early 1920's, October has meant a visit from the Skullhunters, who wreak havoc on the school in the lead up to Devil's Night, which is comparatively a safe, chaste, and wacky time.

Lunch today is KIND bars in a big pile. Thank you, anonymous alumni donor!

Doctor M warns us to use every precaution over the next two days since October 1st falls on a weekend, so we are not certain when the Skullhunters will first strike. SFS has been placed on Omega Alert and faculty have been armed with runes and ward books from the restricted wing of the library. The protective armor shutters have been partly lowered over the athletics building.

That is all. Have a safe, safe, safe day, Paranormal School!

[Cole Abrams]

Nat, something is up, and I think our group chat is being monitored. Can you meet me after fourth period?

Cole and Nat

[Natalie Lavigne]

Of course.

[Natalie Lavigne] [secret diary]

> Millie,
> Well, Doctor M won't let us put it in a report or a journal, but Cole and I stopped the first Skullhunters prank. It was a bad one. They had made it so the school would have been shrunk by ten percent—just enough that bags and boxes would hit doorframes and the tallest of us (like Cole!) would have had a terrible time just going up stairs and using lockers and getting around.
> The truth is, I had maybe been avoiding Cole the last couple of days. I didn't know what to do. I mean, I didn't completely avoid him. I texted him a lot, especially to try and get the last part of that water control fish joke.
> Maybe it was more or less business as usual then?
> I got the note from Cole on here, and he was right. There was someone extra listed in our group chat on my phone. Probably that statuesque gremlin Camille Flay or her little brother. So, we met out on the track and it was easy to see that something was off with the Edendale illusion field. The sky was wobbly in the wrong way. A quick look outside in the neighborhood, and there were mysterious new Little Libraries standing at every corner. You know what those are, right? The little boxes that have a shelf for you to leave and take books? There are only three li'l libraries in this neighborhood. The area can't sustain any more. I've traded books at all of them. We are at peak li'l library. These fake ones had some dark purpose.

Cole offered his hand, and I took it (quiet, Millie) and he hoisted me up on top of the little stand thing. From there I could see the thin tendrils of energy snaking up and out to the left of right. The libraries were connected, and they were also forming a pyramid of energy over the school.

Once we saw what was going on it was easy to disrupt the beams. Mrs. Konrath detonated each li'l library in an opaque containment field. They popped like fireworks would, and she compressed the barriers into little cubes she put into her super cool canvas knapsack.

And then, she turned to us, said that we did look cute together, and walked off, leaving us alone at the corner of Coronado and Reservoir.

And that is when things got interesting.

[Cole Abrams]

So, um, I guess I should say something. An announcement. Nat and I are not SFS partners any more. I'll team up with Louis, and Nat will work on a special project of incredible importance to our safety.

Don't worry, she and I are still friendly. We just agreed that this was the best move. Grace the Secretary took the news really hard, so I figured I should post something.

[Natalie Lavigne]

Sir,

Your post about the events of yesterday is pretty vague. Don't you think you should mention that we were joking previously about a secret romance? And don't you think you should mention that you said you just wanted to be friends and then kissed me?

Did that slip your mind? Did you forget? Partner?

Former partner?

Cole and Nat

[Cole Abrams]

Former Partner,

While you are telling them about that conversation maybe you should also say that you also kissed me. That there was another kiss and that one was all your fault! And also, that you say you are joking about things but you really aren't.

I liked being partners, but I don't think we should anymore. I think the reasons are obvious.

[Natalie Lavigne]

Sir,

I don't see any reasons anywhere. You never explained that part.

Hello?! Are you going to give me a cold shoulder? The Cole-d shoulder? I thought I could trust you.

[Louis Air]

Hey, I don't know where you two are but answer your phones!

Edit: Or maybe look out the window. While you two were arguing, the Skullhunters struck again.

Skullhunters

[Alexa Garcia]

A front came through today. It was windy and the temperature dropped a lot and I wish I had remembered a jacket. On the way home, it was gray skies, and the palm trees were waving and leaves and stuff were blowing all over the place.

I can hear the wind hitting my window now. WOOSH!

So. Uh, I should bring back Weird Thing of the Day because today to get to the school I had to climb seven flights of stairs? Just these creepy concrete stairs that appeared when I went through the gate that there was no way around.

Is this going to keep happening?

Skullhunters

[Camila Flay]

We got off to a rocky start, but I think you all saw the gates today. I told you I'd keep my word.

For those of you who are new, for the next month, this school belongs to the Skullhunters. If you see a human, ghost or adult wearing a piece of clothing with a skull on it, just steer clear. We've got important business to do. Business that involves chaos and its proximity to this school.

Deal with it.

[Pleeb Ymambo]

The Skullhunters can go suck on a streetlamp. Every single October, they ruin the rad spooky vibe with a nightmare waterfall of evil pranks. First time, they set up a spacial resonator in the common area across from the office and we had angry ghosts in knickers from New York complaining about homework and how bright the sun was. Then they did the thing where opening a classroom door formed a brick wall over another doorway somewhere else on campus. I got caught in one of those instant walls and had to spend the day with the nurse, phasing brick dust out of my arm.

Ugh, and don't get me started on last year.

[Bobby Flay]

Come one come all to the final performance of Nancy Jairob's hit half-musical, *CATS on a Hot Tin Roof*.

Yes, I know you're going to make a joke, Nancy only wrote the first half as a musical. The rest is straight talking and moving around a stage and going to a little counter to get booze out of a crystal decanter. Get it out of your system now because the PS13 Theatre Troupe is only doing this one last show, Friday at seven!

[Gryphon Flay]

Night falls on Echo Park, and we fly.

SKULL

HUNTERS

[Bobby Flay]

Thanks everyone for the awesome time producing *CATS on a Hot Tin Roof*. Many tin roofs were harmed in the process. ;)

Seriously though, it's been so fun to sit up in the tech booth and push buttons to help make the show happen. Everyone was so good! And the late-night Astro Diner runs were totally worth it. I've never drank so much coffee!

And yes, thanks for asking, Mavis. The gash on my arm from the rogue wood screw is fine.

[Kelli Konrath, CEED]

Quick reminder—your family may have a generations-long vow to harass the school every Fall, but perhaps think twice before using any unmarked fire poles or slides or crawlspaces you don't recognize to move around campus, especially between the hours of midnight and one a.m.

Also, yes, please exercise restraint with the pranks. I strongly disliked the one two years ago with the flying axe. Not that it's a contest.

Skullhunters

[GOMEZ]

We run, like we have not run in a year.

A wall of crackly dried branches weaves up into the air, pointy and there's little bits flying off. A freshman twice my size and with a way too small backpack turns, sees the wall crawling after us, and freezes. I grab her and pull, and she finally runs, too, curly hair bouncing.

We drop bags and bicycles, leaving them to be swallowed by the matchstick tunnel of doom that surrounds us. The opening straight ahead is the only way out. Doors to the library. Students inside see us and jam chairs under the pushbars. We are trapped. We hammer on the windows, futile. The branches snatch us up and suspend us in the air.

Somewhere on the other side of this foliage trap, I hear a distinct, shrill laugh. Camila, the oldest of the Flays. She is pleased with this one. My bespoke pinstripe vest is ruined, a thousand little rips and tears. I will have to get another one from Corvax, the immortal tailor. It will cost me another favor.

The Skullhunters have struck again.

Skullhunters

[Xenton X]

It's so mean, this last prank. Javier loved that plant statue. Now it covers like a quarter of the school, and it tries to grab students and faculty and scrapes their bods and rips their clothes.

Isn't Bobby a Skullhunter? The Flays have been coming to PS13 since the 40s. Their name is all over donation plaques in the restricted wing of the library. He has the same pale complexion and big bushy eyebrows. But maybe he doesn't frown as much as Camila and Gryphon, so people don't notice as much?

He has friends and stuff. Maybe someone should talk to them about being friends with a monster!

[Bobby Flay]

I don't know who talked to Mavis and the others but now they are mad at me. Who did that?

Look, yes, I am a Flay. Camila is my sister and Gryphon is my cousin. And yes, they are Skullhunters. But I'm not one! I don't do pranks. They're mean.

My parents may have been Skullhunters, and my grandparents may have been Skullhunters, and everyone I see over the holidays at Skullmas may be a Skullhunter. And I may have, like, a t-shirt that my dad handed down that has the word *SKULLHUNTER* on it, but I am not a Skullhunter.

I just wanna climb on scaffolding and hang lights in the theater, okay?

[Camila Flay]

In honor of my sweet brother Bobby, who is a very good boy, the Skullhunters will be cursing the student parking lot for the next week. Anyone who parks in it will have their car teleported onto a street that is currently being street cleaned, guaranteeing a parking ticket. Then it will teleport back with the ticket.

This stuff will keep happening until November! The Skullhunters strike again! AHAHAHAHA!

[JR Benton]

Good one, Camila! Man, I love how the Skullhunters cause so much trouble every year. Any chance I can come to the next meeting? I have a healthy resume of mean things I've done over the past two years.

To everyone else: Isn't Camila hot?

[Gryphon Flay]

Our cursed parking lot has struck those of you who don't pay attention to the PS13 journals website. I count… fourteen cars that just reappeared with tickets. Nice one!

A ha ha ha ha ha

[Bobby Flay]

Really, everyone, please, please listen to me. I'm not doing the pranks. It's Gryphon and Camila. I was in the light bay all morning with Mavis searching for old, faded bags of chips and other trinkets only an old haunted theater has. Mavis showed me the rooms under the stage where they set up the hookah lounge in the early 2000s. She kept putting "hookah" in quotes?

[Camila Flay]

Baby brother, you leave me no choice. I'm really sorry about this one, but you need to fall in line. Dad's orders.

For those looking to be impressed by our proud lineage, Dad is Deckard Flay, CEED. Yes, that Deckard Flay.

Skullhunters

[JR Benton]

Wow, hey, Camila, that's pretty cool. Deckard Flay is the guy who made that floaty platform so Paranormal School 8 could hover in the air above Buenos Aires. Very dangerous and cool.

Kind of like your pranks, you know what I'm saying? ;)

Look I have a really juicy prank idea lined up. Meet me at lunch and I'll lay it all out for you. You could never in a million years imagine this one. It's a JR Benton original. I just want those black orbs you call eyes to light up with sinister delight.

I can't stop thinking about you.

[Bobby Flay]

I got kicked out of the theatre program.

They said they couldn't run the risk of Nancy's new half-musical, *Annie Get Your The Crucible*, being sabotaged with such a short rehearsal schedule.

One way to look at this is to say, "Well, Dinner Theatre is a mess every year." Another way to look at this is that I am cast out from the one place I felt like I belonged.

I don't know how to explain it anymore. I'm not evil. I just have a sister who is evil and a family who is evil. And really, I'm not sure how evil she actually is. Camila has a gerbil she keeps on her dresser and that thing is so well-fed and fat and happy.

Camila also has a cage in her room for people, but the point is she has the gerbil next to it and it's a little fuzzball.

I'm going to go to that parking lot everyone makes out in and do some thinking. Blegh.

[Camila Flay]

Cheer up, baby brother. I have another gift for you. This stooge who is obsessed with me gave me the greatest prank the Skullhunters have ever attempted. I'm quivering in my black boots just thinking about it.

And it's yours to be a part of. If you like.

[Bobby Flay]

You know what? Fine. If Nancy and the other less accomplished theatre students don't want me, then maybe I'll go somewhere I belong.

I am a Flay, after all.

[JR Benton]

Camila let me touch her boob. I'm so in love. I can't believe we are going to get married.

[GOMEZ]

The whole campus is on lockdown over worries about the next Skullhunters prank. I haven't seen the place this unnerved since I've been here.

When I get nervous (yes, it happens), I retreat to the restricted wing of the library to do some reading about the thing making me nervous. Today's volume is from the Histories series. It's about all the times prank wars in the Paranormal School System (and its predecessors) have caused lasting permanent damage to the Earth, the Internet (not the America Online, the other) and the fabric of reality. It's a fairly thin book, but I think any length of book about the times Paranormal School students have come close to destroying the building blocks of the universe is too long. Most were normal enough—magic and dimensional collapse, curses, and nefarious deals with cosmic beings. One though… one thing on there chilled me to the core.

It was then that I noticed something in the margin of the page. Someone had scribbled a clumsy heart around the letter C in HB pencil lead.

It was JR. I recognize how he draws the letter C from the numerous handwritten notes we used to exchange at Paranormal Junior High. He was different back then.

He knows not what he is about to unleash.

[DOCTOR M]

Students,

This is your principal, Doctor M.

I cannot make it to the awards ceremony honoring those who accomplished great things at the Paranormal School Intramural Psychic Speech Tournament this last weekend. I have an important appointment.

No, I am not avoiding campus because of the danger posed by the Skullhunters. I really do have an appointment.

Thank you.

[Gryphon Flay]

I have good news

Bobby has come to help us finish our ultra-prank and secure his place as one of us.

SKULLhUNtERS

oNE OF us

[Camila Flay]

Little brother, I am so excited you've come to join us.

And to Paranormal School, I say, today is Halloween! The time is nigh. I hope you've prepared yourself for what is to come.

[Ebit Nicole]

TRANSCRIPT OF MORNING ANNOUNCEMENTS FOR TUESDAY, NOVEMBER 1

Good morning PS13! This is Ebit Nicole and Don Chang.

The weather today is sunny and clear. Temperature will be sixty-one degrees.

This day in Paranormal School System history: Did you know that today marks the end of the Skullhunters's reign of terror over PS13? Every year November 1st is celebrated with relief from students and faculty alike. And what's more, due to the actions of brave PS13 student and ex-Skullhunter Bobby Flay, we were spared from this year's horrific Final Prank. All faculty and students are accounted for and we here at the morning announcements are happy that we were not coerced into reporting fake news about how great the Flay family is.

Today we send our best wishes to Bobby Flay, who (even though he was a Skullhunter) heroically stopped the terrible beast. SFS and faculty report the Maw was its name. Bobby stopped its ritual to invoke the Final Prank by flinging himself into its mouth (or maw!) right as a swarm of smaller person-sized creatures crawled out of it. These thin bipedal nightmares had loose gray skin and terrifying frowning white masks. They panicked when the the Maw began to shudder and climbed back inside as students and faculty looked on. What did Bobby do to the inside of that terrible beast?

Today we also remember Camila and Gryphon Flay, who were sucked into the Maw's maw, potentially as a blood debt for the havoc denied it by Bobby's actions? CEED and other paranormal entities will investigate their current location and whether they can return to campus in time to complete their class requirements.

Lunch today is Jell-O and milkshakes, in solidarity of Bobby's inability to eat solid food.

Doctor M says that any students absent yesterday out of fear will not be counted absent, but they will be required to write a five-paragraph essay about what they would have done to save the day had they been in Bobby Flay's position. He is a classic example of a person born of evil who could have just accepted a life of familial acceptance and generational wealth, torturing the less fortunate. But he risked life and limb to do the right thing. May we all have the courage to not just imagine ourselves as the main character of an exciting movie or podcast, but actually follow through like fictional characters do when the chips are down.

That is all. Have a completely relieving day, PS13!

[Nancy Jairob]

Hi, all. Bobby wants you to know that he's recovering just fine, and he appreciates your show of support, though in light of the Maw prank he asks that you stop sending drama masks to him. Frowning white masks are frightening to him now. He was in the mouth part of that giant beast for a long time, and he won't say what it was like.

I don't know about anyone else, but I am so very impressed with Bobby! Not only did he save us all by joining the Skullhunters, but he did so with a performance I think even the most critical of us would classify as pretty solid. I've already made him promise to audition to be in *Annie Get Your The Crucible.* No more will Bobby be relegated to sitting behind a dusty old dimmer board.

I am aware that his now-ghostly pale skin and yellow eyes and his inability to speak (so far) after climbing into the Maw might cause issues, but I am confident in saying that even when he is wrapped head to toe in bandages at the hospital, I am impressed by his staggering presence.

Who knew that we had such a daring thespian in our midst?

[Alexa Garcia]

Okay, here's a cool development. I can make a pie and then throw it. At my little brother. And it splats like whip cream pies are supposed to, and he gets mad like he's supposed to.

Projections have mass and can do stuff in the world! That's not what the textbook says but it's close enough. The textbook goes on and on about the unusual characteristics of projections, like I guess they are imbued with aspects of the projector.

I'm lying here on my bed with my laptop, and I can't think of anything to make. Hmm.

More. Pies.

[Damien Cross]

Winter is just around the corner, which means there's been a lot of warm weather. Los Angeles is a weird city. Sometimes it gets so warm the bugs come out again. Today I walked under an awning and a wasp nest fell out of it and exploded. I had to jump over a car hood and sprint past the Smoothie King. It was good luck there was a fountain and I could jump in it and the wasps were stopped by the water.

On the other hand, it was bad luck that I was on a date with Esmerelda (which was, in itself, a stroke of crazy good luck—she's an upperclassman!). Esmerelda had to trap the wasps in a magic knockoff

Coach purse. I guess it could have gone worse. She uses that purse a lot. Sometimes I wonder if she ever opened it up and dumped it out, what'd come out of it.

What is love? Asking for a friend.

The Bandido Cafe

[MAX Rushmore]

Every morning I head straight to the theatre classroom, vault over the desk, and shoulder roll into Ms. Smith's office like I'm allowed to be in there. I sneak by two theatre seniors making out on the couch and dive into the storeroom where I pour a massive cup of coffee from the pot prepared bi-daily by Nancy Jairob. I slam packet after packet of sugar into that pink paper cup until the coffee is syrupy sweet, and by the time the late bell rings and I'm in my seat in Psychotectonics I've had a liter of this potent dark nectar.

Coffee is life and the concept of a building separate from Ms. Smith's office where one can get as much coffee as they need makes my heart beat really, really fast.

Or that might just be the caffeine.

[Halvo O]

Has anyone else been to the little coffee shop down the street? It's so dimly lit and (dare I say) romantic! I think I'll come here every day to do homework, or maybe on a cool date if Mabel and I set it up! Haha.

The Bandido Cafe

[Mabel Avagyan]

I saw that place the other day, Halvo. I went inside and it smelled like roses, plus fresh paint because I guess it is new? Feels like home, huh?

[Halvo O]

It. Is. A. Date.

I'm going to take Mabel to Bandido's! We're going to study in candlelight after school, bright sunlight shooting squares through windows and into walls. Then maybe, if everything works out, when the squares have begun to cross Mabel's super cute rectangular face, she'll kiss me!

This is the day I have planned.

[Adult Lyle]

Hi, students of PS13. I'm Lyle, and I own Bandido's Cafe on Sunset! We're excited to see you special weird kids coming in. I just wanted to say we love having you! I'll give a discount to any PS student who shows a student ID or can move one of my espresso tampers without touching it (using your powers, of course). Coffee on!

That's my saying. I say, "Coffee on!" after staff meetings so we get amped for serving our customers!

[Mikey12]

I want to say thank you to all my new friends from Bandido's! Sam, Kyle, Mabel, and yeah, even Old Man Lyle who is a big dork (and pretty okay for an old guy). I've never wanted to stick around after school, but I also never had a club to hang out with. Society? Yes. Club, no.

[Sam Mitchmoon]

Whatever, man. It's no big thing

[Kyle Lemley]

Nah, Sam, this is cool. We should respect what Mikey made. Homework Club. We should call it that.

I am a homework machine.

[Mikey12]

If we're talking the new club, why not call it The Homework Society?

You guys are old(er) and huge though, so I'll go along with whatever!

Don't rock the boat, Mikey!

[JR Benton]

What's with all the lovey shit, you guys? I leave school for one week for a *very* good reason, and I come back and people from different cliques are all at coffee like it ain't a thing? What is this?

Mabel, how could you?

[Oliver 181]

Hey, where is everyone? The library is gosh darned vacant. This is fire. I can sit on a table, and no one is even noticing.

Who would ever call the library "fire"?

And yet...

The Bandido Cafe

[Mabel Avagyan]

The bathrooms here at Bandido's smell like the desert. Wind and dry. This is the best place I have ever been to ever. I can hear the electric rhythm guitar just thinking about it.

[Adult Lyle]

Big event, y'all! I made an afternoon special on Tuesdays just for PS13. That's a slow time for us so I figured we could help each other out, you and me. You come in and hang out on the big cushy couch or maybe at the cafe bar with me, and I'll give you a *free* drip coffee with every muffin or croissant you get! That's like half off your muff n coff!

Coffee on!

By the way, do youngs say "amped" anymore? I'm guessing no.

[Vert Merpson]

I walked into Bandido's today and it was the same dark welcoming ambiance as always. I had this fleeting vision, like one of those premonitions psychics get, that something was different today. But Lyle was there, as always, and the espresso was there, as always, and their big chrome hot rod coffee machine made that rattle every five minutes, so I chalked it up to positive energy leftover from the pep rally earlier (go Raccoons!).

And I was so wrong! Because I got my coffee and was sipping the foam off the top and I laid eyes on the most beautiful creature I'd ever seen.

He was a couple of inches shorter than me, with eyes that sort of protruded from a thin face. A Japanese mechanical pencil stuck out of the tuft of curly hair tucked behind an ear. He was up to his eyeballs in homework, senior spellbooks piled high on his table, margins scribbled with runes.

At last, my senior mentor.

Okay, I'm gonna go beg him to tutor me in runecraft.

[Adult Lyle]

A match is made! I guess y'all are supposed to get a senior mentor when you're a junior? I don't know. I'm just glad it happened in these hallowed walls. Joe's wards were worth the trouble to install.

Maybe my role is more hands off. I hadn't really…

Joe, you could be clearer, man. I try to participate in every desert campfire sit-in you warp me to in my sleep.

Thursdays remain open mic night at Bandido!

Coffee on!

[Adult Lyle]

The Paranormal Pastry Happy Hour is a smash! A big success. Y'all are such a great crowd. Really refreshing after the morning rush of people from that tech company office.

Hey, I had another idea!

We've got a back line at Bandido now.

(I'm typing this while I'm lookin at you, BTW.)

I see all y'all loner kids, on your smart tabs and e-phones, sneaking puffs on your sleeve-vapes. New rule! You have to make a friend from the back line to sit there. You don't gotta go to prom together. I just wanna see some life coming outta those high benches along the wall!

Also don't sit on the little separate side tables. I know they are seat height but those aren't seats. Trays go there.

Coffee on!

[Hyper Akeelah]

Excuse me, I am one of this "back line" and I take offense. I am from a dimension made of what one of you "3-D" entities would call clouds. It is so solid and heavy here. My only respite is an opportunity to turn off my extensive (very extensive) social training and just be for a microt.

[Enid, Often Alone]

I have friends, really. That's mean, Lyle. The name on here was a joke name.

[Alexa Garcia]

Seriously, coffee shops are there so you can do homework and read Tumblr in relative peace. I don't need a buddy!

[Adult Lyle]

Okay! Okay. I'm sorry back line crowd. You don't have to be social if you don't want. I just... okay, look. Just consider—*consider*—for a minute that it might be a little fun to connect with a human. Hey, if I'd never talked to a stranger before I wouldn't have met my business partner, Shadow Joe!

[Sam Mitchmoon]

Shadow Joe sounds like a made-up person.

[Kyle Lemley]

Yeah, like a Canadian significant other. If Joe exists, what does he look like? Then again, I have a twin with almost exactly my name and people don't believe he is real.

[MAX Rushmore]

You guys are gonna jinx this oasis. Just slam that coffee.
    Just thinking about the cafe makes me start doing big karate moves, like I'm watching a movie. I wish I was there now. It's a crime I'm not. I'm so angry I am not there.

[Alexa Garcia]

Life continues.

Oh, I made a list of things I'm supposed to learn to stop Lurkett and I'm more confused than when I started.

1. Psychic mind-fighting
2. Flight (the hero psychic could fly)
3. Anti-magic jujitsu?
4. Time travel?
5. Learn what a Titan is but no one will tell me?

At this point I don't even understand how they know what her name was, but apparently the firsthand reports from witnesses said she (Lurkett) yelled something like "cupid lurkett" so the name stuck.

Honestly Cupid as a first name isn't the worst.

Ugh, anyway.

An Infestation

[Ebit Nicole]

TRANSCRIPT OF MORNING ANNOUNCEMENTS FOR FRIDAY, DECEMBER 2

Good morning PS13! This is Ebit Nicole and Don Chang.

The weather today is sunny and clear. Temperature will be sixty degrees.

This day in Paranormal School System history: It's Curse Day! December 1st is an important date for many students at the Paranormal School System, as many curses and prophecies use the eX Calendar (which starts way back in 2002), and December 1st is the last day of the year in that one. If you know of someone who has been cursed, ask politely if today is the day is they are finally free!

Lunch today is pizza circles.

Please note that Doctor M will make a special announcement at nine a.m.

That is all. Have a safe, productive day, Paranormal School!

An Infestation

[DOCTOR M]

TRANSCRIPT OF PUBLIC ADDRESS ANNOUNCEMENT
(Transcribed by Grace the Secretary)

Hello, students. This is your principal.

Your PS13 teachers and administrators are aware of the presence of several supernatural, mirrored gateways on campus that appear late at night. Some appear to be mirrored automatic doors like a department store might have, some are shiny fire poles that drop into a void, and some are (apparently) exciting-looking, chrome "fun slides."

None of you are even supposed to be here late at night, but I know how it goes when you receive a mysterious letter from your missing father or aunt or whatever. In the interest of safety, I have chosen to break from Paranormal School System policy and explain what these are.

These doors connect to a place we call the Internet (short for Psychic Internetwork), a network of pocket dimensions that intersect with and mirror our world.

It has no relation to the electronic computer network we use on our phones and personal computers.

The pocket dimensions that make up the Internet (again, not the other one) are dangerous and warped reflections of our own, but they also have important, practical uses. They are what allow psychics to think at each other, cubes to become hypercubes, and magic users to channel the moon/sun/etc. Despite its many unpleasant and frightening aspects, this endless catacomb of almost-reality is as much a part of our world as the sky.

While gateways into the Internet appear throughout the world, there are an unusually high number around the campuses of the Paranormal School System due to the extreme concentration of weirdness at our schools. It is sort of like how power lines crackle in Los Angeles, because of all the electricity being used here.

Actually, that's a terrible example. Never mind.

The Internet can also... hm.

Now I'm confused. But it's Friday and I need the student body to be properly warned about the incredible danger that lies below us all.

Hang on. Let me think.

[long pause]

Okay, what if we keep calling the computer internet 'the Internet' and we call this Psychic pocket dimension network the Matrix? Because it is a subworld matched to our own and has many matrices. Aspects you can step between if you...

[short pause]

It has nothing to do with the media franchise of the same name but at least the Matrix is a slightly less used term than 'the Internet.'

The Matrix (the Internet) is very dangerous. Many areas do not follow the same rules as our physical world, and strange and deadly entities lurk in nooks beyond sight.

Other areas are endless labyrinths... uh, but not to be confused with our own Infinite Labyrinth and school mascot, the raccoon "A-Maze-o."

The Matrix mazes are full of bizarre and confounding death traps. A-Maze-o by contrast is...

You know what? I was going to make a joke. Let's move on.

It is official school policy that students are forbidden from entering the Matrix without a certification from CEED, the Cross-discipline Exploration and Emergency Directorate. None of you are thirty and wearing a badge and a sleek, black jumpsuit so there will be no tolerance for those who break policy.

Students who attempt to enter the Matrix will be harshly punished, up to and including unpleasant ideas pulled from 19th century educational guidebook, *The Flogged Young Wizard*. If one of you got erased from history Grace would never forgive me.

Alright, announcement made.

[loud clattering]

They're going to get themselves killed.

[short pause]

Yeah, this announcement was a mistake. I'm so confused.

An Infestation

I hit the button, what do you mean it's still—
[announcement broadcast ends]

[MAX Rushmore]

So, this isn't the one from the movies, right?

[Corey Yuiop]

Okay, who else is going to come with me tonight to sneak into the Matrix (the Internet)? This is gonna be so fun!

[Mikey12]

I'm in. Damien?

[Damien Cross]

I don't know man. Maybe. Seems risky.

[JR Benton]

I'm coming, too, boys! You can't keep a party animal like me away from a good time!

[Mikey12]

Wow! Okay, cool. Never hung out with an upperclassman before. How do we get in?

[JR Benton]

What?

[Damien Cross]

Mikey hasn't so much as acknowledged that his club fell apart because he was being a punk. Or that his homework club at the coffee place fell apart (I heard about that the other day).

Now all he does is talk about what it's like to turn into a werewolf and shred on a chunk of tree trunk his dad brought him.

The truth is I've been going into this Matrix place every Sunday night for a couple of hours. I've got a loose map of the first dozen rooms in a couple of directions.

Is a habit still good if you can't not do it?

[Monika M]

I got a letter from my friend Micah today. He sends letters by miniature porcelain courier through the Matrix because a (smallish) clockwork courier can cover the five thousand miles between here and Copenhagen in only fifteen minutes if they know the right path through the rooms.

In Denmark, we are allowed into several pockets of the Matrix, which we call the Gardens. Which I guess doesn't make much sense as the areas I know of look like flooded subway stations. Honestly, they're pretty disturbing, but when you grow up playing in ankle-deep black water in a room made entirely of white tile, you do not consider it so strange?

Micah sent pictures of our friends out biking in Copenhagen and it made me really angry. Why do I have to be here when all my friends—even sweet, delicious Micah—are over there? Why do I have to miss them having fun?

[Natalie Lavigne]

Students for Safety's official stance is and always has been that the Matrix/the Internet and its myriad strange pocket dimensions are to be kept secret from the student body. It's obvious that more students going into the Matrix is just going to cause more problems.

If anyone really wants a chance to look at this forbidden nightmare maze, why don't you come to the SFS orientation today during 6th period? We've got a bunch of VHS tapes CEED made of a doomed expedition in the 90s. Watch as a guy in camo with a huge axe gets swallowed by a living doorway! And his cries for help can be heard in the walls of other rooms!

[Louis Air]

Nat, I think maybe we shouldn't show freshmen those tapes. They're really disturbing.

[GOMEZ]

Funny story! I have been taking a shortcut through the Matrix on my walk to school for the last three school years.

You know those tunnels that go under the street, so you don't have to run across traffic or go to a crosswalk? Well, I thought I was using one of those, but I ended up walking home late today and it was completely gone. Instead of a stairwell that led to a gated tunnel, there was just a brick wall and the back door of some pizza place.

This morning the door I use was back. As was the cloaked figure that blocks the tunnel entrance every morning. It seemed to grow in front of me, tattered gray robes like a thick fog enveloping the tunnel until there was nothing but a glistening green mouth wafting black vapor.

"Good morning!" I said.

"Your soul, if you fail," it hissed.

It handed me a piece of paper with a riddle on it. I answered the riddle (it was toadstools) and the thing swept aside, and I came to on the ground on the other side of Sunset Boulevard.

I guess that's a room in the Matrix. I had no idea.

[Xenton X]

Gomez, you're saying you have a daytime Matrix shortcut? Aren't they only nighttime though?

[GOMEZ]

You're right. Hm. Well, who knows what that tunnel is then. Never mind!

[JR Benton]

Okay, kittens (and kats and babes and dudettes):.

I found a choice gateway into the Matrix, and we are for sure going. It's got a big sign taped above a tube slide (no water, a dry one) that says, "To a Big Fun Time!" I can see the casino now.

Me and the guys will be leading that squad of feral cats from the neighborhood into a matrix door tonight. Be there or be square. Who is coming?

EDIT: Okay, okay. I'll see myself meowt. You're missing out though! It's gonna be a blast.

[Mikey12]

Okay, we're going into the Matrix later. I'll let you know how it goes. I don't think there's going to be cats. I think that was what JR calls a "JR-ism."

[Alexa Garcia]

Everyone is flipping out about the Matrix doors. I've never seen the school so focused on one thing. It sounds like there's going to be some extra security here at night now, but it hasn't stopped many students.

I hear some of the gateways look like really shiny house doors. I

An Infestation

wonder if my little house up on the hill's door appears at night. Does it disappear from its place at the front of that house when it does?

I guess in hindsight they were teaching us in Introduction to the Mind about the Matrix, since that's what psychic energy channels through. But it seemed benign enough when we were looking at the psychic stuff. Crystal caves, purple creeks, you know. Elf stuff.

What's so dangerous about this place when you go there in person? There's no way it's just mazes and traps.

[Damien Cross]

That was wild.

An Infestation

[Mikey12]

Okay, that was incredibly boring, except for the end. That place is 100% just a concrete maze.

We were in a place like two hundred feet underground and every single room was just metal doors and crusty old concrete walls.

I wanted to leave immediately on account of... um, how this looked like the maintenance room in a parking garage, and that sounds like boring. But Damien was going on and on about how his uncle told him to solve mazes.

Apparently you pick a wall and just move like you are keeping a hand on that wall and if you follow it around, you will come out the other side and Win the MAZE!

But the Matrix doesn't go anywhere! We must have done the left wall thing for a solid hour and then we looped around to the start. So, we tried the right-hand wall and then we somehow ended up touching the left wall again?

JR started freaking out at that point for some reason, but Corey assured us we could figure this out if we just stopped following a wall. But then we got lost and Corey changed into a wendigo (arctic deer monster) and a bunch of sharp antlers came out of his arms, and we had to run. That was the part I said wasn't boring.

JR demanded I turn into a werewolf, but I told him it doesn't work like that (gotta be feeling that moonbeam). And then Damien jump kicked the Coreymonster.

Damien got the monster by crunching him in a big trap door thing and we get out of the maze just as the gateway back to campus was closing.

All in all, a somewhat exciting adventure. Not super interesting in total.

Okay, fine. The Corey thing is weird. I remember Corey being at school, but I guess he never was except for the day of the announcement. I have memories of the time he dared me to smoke one of my dad's cigarettes. And my dad doesn't smoke. Definitely no way he doesn't. He's a librarian.

[Monika M]

I've completely had it!

Micah was teasing me with Snaps of every bike bridge in Copenhagen, and he sent me one of Cykelslangen (which is a cool-looking bridge) and I just got up and walked out of school and walked home and started packing. If a stupid letter about how great Micah looks with a haircut can get here in fifteen minutes through the ether, then I can get there at the same time.

There's a fire pole with a big neon sign that says, "To The Fun House" that opens at the back of the 100 building that no one knows about, says JR.

[Alexa Garcia]

I think I just saw Monika spooking through my backyard. Am I supposed to do something?

[DOCTOR M]

Daily step count: 15,029

Multiple students have chosen to disobey school orders and go into the Matrix (the Internet) unprepared. Now we have a missing student. Monika Marquadt (who I share a kinship with for difficult to pronounce M surnames) was seen on security cameras clouding the minds of the contract security guards and sliding down a reflective fire pole into the Matrix on campus early this morning.

I have warned them, Grace. I have warned them about books that breathe fire and melting escalators. I have warned them about vortexes and lightning that isn't lightning and about the Titans and about the dangers of thinking too hard when using a wide range of innocent-seeming supernatural powers.

I told them not to ask questions to the statue at the northwest corner of the building or to talk to anyone that looks exactly like them. And I told them to avoid stairwells and doorways during an earthquake (because that is an old earthquake myth and is very dangerous).

But they just don't listen. And I just pulled up Monika's journal and she was doing it all for a bike path. I'm going to smoke an e-cig with the theoretical math teachers. We all have reason to.

[Cole Abrams]

Nat,

Have you heard anything from the school about what they're doing to go after that student? I saw Ms. Konrath today and she didn't seem to be doing anything but teaching.

[Natalie Lavigne]

I didn't. And it's Mrs. Konrath. She got married last month.

[Cole Abrams]

Thank you so much for the correction.

Damien Cross approached my team today, and he thinks he knows where Monika is.

[Alexa Garcia]

I can't believe that Monika really was the girl I saw. I could have said something to her when she was going through my back yard. I could have—I don't know—made a projection of a bear claw (the pastry) in front of her and I could have talked to her.

Ah, who am I kidding? I wouldn't have done that.

I'm really worried about her.

[Mikey12]

Why don't we just go into the door she went in and go get her?

[Damien Cross]

No way. Mikey that is a terrible idea. We almost got eaten by a muscular eight-foot-tall deer that pretended to be a lifelong friend but wasn't. <u>It led us in there!</u>

I told SFS, so hopefully they're going to do something about it. They were all at their room when I walked by today. I told them we know the area Monika was in because we rode the same fire pole. The sign says it goes to a fun house, but that's not very representative of what's actually down there. Both from a fun perspective and a house perspective.

Leave it to the pros, man.

[Kelli Konrath, CEED]

The on-call SFS team just recovered Monika from campus this morning. It's a miracle she's okay, aside from some lingering paranoia. I'm awaiting the SFS team's reports to sit down with Doctor M. It might be time to send word up the chain at CEED. There's no way I could authorize students to head in there and still look at myself in my app-driven workout mirror.

EDIT: Just now we've determined Mikey Doze is missing. Good grief. Hang on.

[Sven Kovalik]

Is Mikey really missing? Check inside the shed with the dodgeballs and Psytag stuff.

An Infestation

[Kelli Konrath, CEED]

Here's a rhetorical question: How many "incidents" have to happen before your average Paranormal School student decides a place is too dangerous? Two? Ten?

I guess I get it. Paranormal School students are powered by curiosity. I know I was when I was a student back in the late 90s and there was the hedge maze incident at the old Manor House. There's always something. Some big ominous lever to pull.

Mikey Doze and Monika M seem to have found a particularly dangerous corner of the Internet. Sorry, the Matrix. It's inhabited by a creature named the Cormorant, according to a record of dangerous Matrix critters from tomes in the restricted wing of the library.

We did some research (thank you, Annabelle), and the Cormorant is an ageless entity that is able to get into our world from its Matrix dimension. Not sure how it does it, but it's extremely convincing when it shows up and says it's your old sparring partner or what have you.

Its lair looks like an old 1970s parking garage, IMO. It lures you in and it can bend the rules enough that it's basically impossible to get out. Those boys were extraordinarily lucky they had a Lucksmith* with them when they went in the first time. Without him or even the basic safety skills of a solid-C student like JR Benton, I fear Mikey would...

Now that I'm reading this, I wish this stupid journaling software would let you delete posts.

---

*That's the best way any of the faculty has come up with to describe young Damien Cross's penchant for just barely surviving any physical action he takes, no matter how dangerous.

[Mikey12]

Do you get extra credit for saving the day? I should get some extra credit. Maybe Damien, too, I guess since he helped me learn this Matrix Zone or whatever it's called. I was able to get Monika out while the Coreymonster was looking for us, but he split us up and I ran so he would chase me, and Monika could get out.

I'm still in here.

I'm holding my phone up to the corner of this one specific hallway, at about two-thirds of the way between one flickering cracked fluorescent light thingy and a scratched message that reads, "COREY WAS HERE." There's one bar on my phone. So, I got the page to load and if you can read this, I guess I got the bar again. I'm low on juice. Gotta save the other percents for the light.

Can anyone come get me? I'm not far in. The pole is too slick to climb up.

Come get me, please! Please? Hello?

[Monika M]

Alright. I'm okay and back in LA. I promise not to try and sneak home through means other than plane flights and magical portals.

[Alexa Garcia]

I'm so glad Monika is okay, but... is she okay? She seems pretty spooked. I went to go sit with her at lunch and she just sort of recounted the events of the newest season of *Euphoria*. She'd been watching *Euphoria*, yes, but she didn't used to just spout out facts about the episode. There was something else there.

[Natalie Lavigne]

Ladies and gentlemen and enbys, since the little throwdown today with a certain witch has caused some disturbed questions, I would like to explain a little bit about how I work.

The Dimensionally abled have the ability to interact with the world around them in unusual ways (thanks to the ability to hop in and outta here). Wizards and witches can sometimes do similar things, through what are essentially promises made and extracted from the entities that hold the universe together. I don't have that problem.

Uh, with the universe, anyway.

Those of us with what the school categorizes as "dimensional" powers don't technically have any special abilities. We just happen to be from somewhere with very different rules. I know there's only a few of us here, which is maybe why this isn't well-known.

So, what does all that mean? I can blink myself in and out of the present in short bursts, and when I'm not "here," I can see a lot of stuff in a seemingly normal room that is not normal. Just building blocks of the universe stuff.

The really fun part is, with enough practice (thank you, Annabelle), I'll be able to make stable slipstream folds that I and other people can move through. Real, actual portals. It's a top priority this year.

See? Rumors are untrue.

The Notebook

LIBRARY RESTRICTED ZONE SAFETY CABINET INVENTORY

ARTICLE 112-2

"The Notebook"

Check this box if this requires normal inspections by Students for Safety [X]

Appearance: A Velcro-sealed three-ring student binder from the late 1980s, featuring irritated-looking neon dolphins rendered in blue, green and pink in front of an indigo rainbow starfield. Originally used by a ███████████████████ to keep ███████████████████ ████████ for the ███████████ (go Raccoons!).

Divergence: [Original notation] The Notebook behaves erratically.

[Updated notation, on third page] Notebook operates across

The Notebook

time and space as if sentient, empowered with the skills and experience of a master Vector Apocryphant?

[Updated notation, on final page] Notebook cannot be destroyed but must be.

Timeline of incidences:

/1998

When dropped by a student in Mr. Cromworp's Social Studies class, Notebook would spray papers containing future pop quizzes. Duplicates from the Notebook exactly matched the Word files on Mr. Cromworp's classroom computer.

■■/■■/1998

When Velcro seal is broken in the cafeteria, The Notebook emanates notebook paper covered with doodles of the sat contents of an entire row of lunch tables, with extra doodles of pizza and pizza-adjacent products (pizza pocket, etc).

■■/■■/1998

When containing the mystical Victorian compass artifact "The Eye of the West Indies," the Notebook creates two perfectly sharpened No.2 pencils inside the clear "pencil zone" bag on the inside of the front cover.

Placing a pencil inside the compass artifact causes a correct geometry answer to appear on all geometry tests in the same room.

Attempting to turn in stapled papers labeled "Geometry Test" creates sharpened No.2 pencils, completed tests (all answers correct), and an identical copy of the Notebook on all desks in a ~90-meter radius.

Paranormal School 13

The Notebook copies are destroyed, and the original is confiscated from the student, ███████████. Student claims it was a "hand me down from my sister, why would I have a Trapper Keeper with dolphins on it?"

███/███/1998

The Notebook is removed from the Safety Cabinet by rogue students. It is recovered when juniors ███████ and ███████████ use it to attempt to disrupt printing of the infamous mid-semester UltraQuiz in Mrs. Ehrlenroy's Psychotectonics class.

Placing The Notebook inside Mrs. Ehrlenroy's desk overnight causes all classwork for the year to be immediately created, printed, filled in, graded, returned to students (evidenced by additional wear, doodles, folds, and wrinkles), thrown away around campus or filed away, and the final grades entered into the campus computer server.

Despite distinct handwriting and student-accurate performance, neither teacher nor students recall doing the years' worth of classwork.

███/███/1999

When a lesson plan (in this case, for Neural Mapping), is placed inside The Notebook, all teaching staff on campus immediately feel an overwhelming burst of jubilant relief, that the school year has just ended after months of challenging, rewarding work. Staff all has detailed memory of hard-fought wins with troubled students, challenging days during test season, and big moments in personal life and pop culture.

In the ensuing melee, the Notebook is destroyed by ███████████.

BRARY RESTRICTED ZONE SAFETY CABINET IN\

ARTICLE 112-2
"The Notebook"

██/██/1999

The Notebook reappears in the Library Restricted Zone Safety Cabinet, only sign of damage from the gout of flame that destroyed it is one of the vinyl seams is slightly warped and torn, revealing the cardboard interior of the front cover.

██/██/1999

"Loaning" the Notebook from one student to another causes The Notebook to fill with 185 pages of blank, lined notebook paper, regardless of current contents of the Notebook. "Loaning" actions include handing the Notebook to another, throwing the Notebook, opening the Notebook, closing the Notebook, or even just leaving it on the ground for one minute.

By the time SFS recaptures the Notebook, the school accumulates an eight-year supply of notebook paper.

██/██/1999

In physical education classes, opening and closing the velcro on the Notebook causes the wielder to gain the health benefits of approximately six week's worth of consistent muscle and endurance exercise.

When placed back in the Safety Cabinet, the Notebook now features a muscular princess drawn in ballpoint pen on the teal vinyl of the inside back cover.

██/██/1999

During the Second Clocksmen Attack, opening the Notebook in the direction of ███ ███████████ ██████ caused hundreds of

The Notebook

████████████████████████ to fall from the sky (space?) and disable the Clocksmen's ███████████, ███████████.

███/███/1999

When the Notebook is placed in any backpack in room 241 on the PS13 campus, any student wearing any Paranormal School letter jacket (tested: PS13, PS3, PS18), would immediately graduate (student database updated with final grades, certificate appears in student home) and age fourteen years.

Aging is reversible using a ███████ cast by ███████ ███████████.

███/███/1999

The ███████████ ███████████ creates a temporal ban of the Notebook, but the Notebook was not in the Safety Cabinet at the moment of the ban. It was in the possession of plucky student investigator Iris Blankstrom, who ███████████ ███████████.

SFS recovered Iris from a ███████████ ███████████ in low earth orbit in ████████.

███/███/1999 - ███/███/2000

It is discovered several months into the school year that the Notebook has been entered into the student database as a new student (class of '00). The Notebook appears numerous times in 99-00 school year paperwork and records, including as a ███████ ███████████, ███████ ███████████, and ███████ ███████████.

While documentation from this era is spotty, it is clear this year was rife with minor disturbances and several alumni still reference the Notebook's reputation for ███████████ ███████████ in private.

Paranormal School 13

At the end of the year, staff elect to update the Notebook's student record so that it "graduates" from PS13.

During the Graduation Day ceremony, the Notebook ███ ███ ████████ when the actual ████████, ████ ██████, fell ill from food poisoning (unrelated coincidence). The speech was delivered with ████ ████ ████ and eloquently waxed romantic on ████ ████ ████ ████ ████████ (both terms were used), pleaded for forgiveness for ███ █████████ █████ ██████ ██████ ██████, and went on a several minute long, awkward diatribe about █████ ████ ████ ████ ████ █████ with fellow student ███ ████████.

The Notebook has not been seen on campus since Graduation Day, 2000.

[Alexa Garcia]

Someone <u>finally</u> explained to me what a Titan is. Which Lurkett was/is?

In case you didn't know, a Titan is a person who, through supernatural means, has transcended their humanity in a way that makes them very dangerous. Some are very old, like Argos the Destroyer (who used to be a fisherman named Tim). And some are relatively new, like Lurkett, who is some kind of incorporeal shade that could slam stuff with giant storms made of terrifying faces. Yep, I actually finally learned who/what Lurkett is, and I'm still reeling.

The theory is (no one knows) Lurkett was a Paranormal School student. And the theory is she found something she shouldn't have (theory is, a book of cursed magic) and went rogue and attacked the city for some reason.

There was a SFS student nearby who tried to stop her, along with a CEED emergency response team and local authorities, but it got very bad and eventually other entities had to get involved. She had unleashed this crazy energy burst, and even though everyone tried, they weren't able to contain it and it caused these disturbances that even went out into the city and caused a huge earthquake. (!)

So, I'm supposed to stop her? How?! I can barely put a tube around a light bulb and trap the light.

This is stressing me out.

[GOMEZ]

One cool thing about having a curse is you can go see the nurse any time there's a flare-up.

The Dance

[Mikey12]

I am alive! And I am back!

I made my way up out of the Matrix through a gateway in a place called the Window Swamp, which is a couple of zones over from the parking garage with the arctic deer monster in it. I werewolfed up through a yellow-framed mirror suspended in the air, and into the waiting arms of the clear, Southern California night sky (and all the cute little hills with the houses in them!). Oh, how I've missed you, LA.

Never thought I'd say that. But hey, I'm a changed man. Reconnected with my wolf side down there and everything. Not only can I change into a werewolf on command, but I can also <u>not</u> change back! You could say I'm Mikey13 now! Get it? Maybe if they ever update this ancient website, they'll make it so we can change our names. Might help some of the other students like me who maybe weren't listening carefully when they had us make our login.

I really should get home so I can check in with my Dad, but since I had to walk by campus to get to my bus, I thought I'd stop in to check out the announcements board.

And the dance is coming!

Gosh, it's in like a week. I don't remember the exact date. I guess I got back after midnight and the school was locked up. There were a lot of adult security people, ones with night vision goggles and eerily quiet dogs that don't bark. So, I hustled off to find some pants (wolf mode tears my pants).

Um, does anyone want to go to the dance with me? Fair warning: I'm a lot taller and werewolf-shaped, but I know someone's gonna be down with that! Down with Mikey13!

[Alexa Garcia]

After much pressure from Monika and Mikey (who is now a huge wolf monster), I have agreed to go to the Winterween dance. And I don't want to hear about the "true" name of the dance. I can't pronounce it.

I'll be there with bells on! Literally. That's how I go. To dances. Which I am an expert at.

[Kelli Konrath, CEED]

I need some extra hours, so the school approved my chaperoning the dance. I got away with a lot at the Winterween Dance in my day, so this should give me an edge when uncovering... antics.

[Phoebe Case]

Oh. My. God.

The dance is almost here! I was crushed when homecoming came and went, but it turns out this school has dances after all. I mean, of course it does. All high schools have dances. From the very fancy to the very normal. Even homeschooled kids like moi had dances. Yes, I got invited to my first good conduct dance when I was thirteen! The boy's name was Emory, and he was dreamy. Like, in thirteen-year-old dreamy ways. I wrote him a detailed and lengthy message on AOL Instant Messenger about why I was so excited by this moment.

It didn't work out. Anyway. You'd better believe I'll be there taking notes and having a blast.

Someone ask me to the dance!

[Natalie Lavigne]

Sir,

I'm sorry I haven't been around much at SFS. Really, I'm sorry. The last month of Advanced Decahedral Navigation is really something. Torreflot (not *Miss* Torreflot, just Torreflot, thank you—which she says like thirteen times a week) has us collapsing facets so that we can pass hard candies and other regional snacks to students at PS9. Problem is, no one has managed to do it and doing the trick right is ten percent of our final grade.

That one investigation is also really something. Harp fills what gaps I have. The parents are even around more.

Still, I miss your towering presence and intellect and calm voice.

Will you be my date for the dance? I could use a partner in socializing. ;)

[Cole Abrams]

I had to run across campus today. There was this little gold sparkling thing flitting around. It looked like a magical sports ball from a popular magic adventure book series. But every time this little bugger stopped next to paper or anything flammable, it would light it on fire.

SFS had actually sent two teams to deal with it, but the first had got distracted by a teacher. Apparently, Louis hadn't turned in homework in several days. The second was waylaid because Ms. Cartwright has curtains in the windows of her classroom and those were on fire from the little gold ball.

So, I chased it through the 300 building and across the track. It never flew more than about twelve feet in the air. Eventually, it got low enough I could grab it. In between its little baby bursts of fire, I inspected it. It turns out it was a living Oscars/Academy Awards statue without the base. In its hands were what appeared to be a can of hair

The Dance

net and a tiny lighter. The butt said "made in Vietnam" but beyond that the little guy wouldn't answer any questions.

It goes into the Safety Cabinet with those hypercubes.

[GOMEZ]

Did anyone else see that huge, jet-black bird with four wings swoop in and snatch up the squirrel today during the assembly outside? The one with Detective Johnson and the liaison from the Office of Naval Intelligence?

I don't think they should have fired their guns at it as it flew away, but no one said anything, and I doubt they'll get in trouble. I think we would have done the same. I've never seen teachers scream like that.

I can tell I'm going to have nightmares about the bird tonight.

Pretty excited for the dance though.

[Cole Abrams]

And yes, Nat. I'll be your date for the dance. I think that'd be really fun. I will have to figure out an outfit. I don't fit into my vest and shirt from last year.

I remember Torreflot's candy test. It wasn't easy I guess.

[Mabel Avagyan]

The giant terrifying four-winged black bird is in my class.

Today it was called on to answer an incredibly hard question about Twin Reality Thermodynamics.

It got it right
It got it rioiiioiooght

Paranormal School 13

The Bird - artist unknown

The Dance

[Nouto Hashimoto]

Okay, I am almost done layering spells into my dress. I followed the plans to the letter. I got a discarded wedding dress, had it tailored, removed the sleeves, and used strips of cloth from the cursed cocktail dress, Marybeth, to add some color to the bustier part. Since then, every day at three a.m. I've set an alarm so I can wake up and read a haiku to the dress while it gestates on its hanger.

> *I'm here, Marybeth*
> *Think of all my hopes and dreams*
> *Make my dancing great*

This dance is going to be fire.

[Kyle Lemley]

Does anyone know if the four-winged giant crow monster has a date to the dance?

[Synthea Fluffson]

Is anyone going to skip dates for Winterween? Dates are always the worst. Let's just go to this dance and have some fun. Cut a rug, my mom says. No tears on a Saturday, she also says!

No idea what either of those mean.

[Natalie Lavigne]

Sir,

Ooh, a new outfit! Now is your chance to impress with something exotic, like an ascot. How are your sisters, by the way?

[Cole Abrams]

Ah, yes. Here, just for you, is an update.

Mina: Has expressed interest in Girl Scouts (Brownies?) and now has acquired a sash from somewhere. Really, we don't know where she got it. Lots of patches. Maybe a mystery to solve there when you're done with all your other projects.

Margo: Big fan of the new *Little Puddlejumpers Sing the Hits* volume. Over and over, at top volume.

Malia: Pulled her off the top branch of our tree earlier. Accuses me of "keeping her grounded" but I think she means more literally. Also, that's a bad thing, according to her.

Mel: She spends an awful lot of time staring at me from the end of the hallway. Harry, I think, is starting to get a little worried about her. She asks if she can come inside at the doorway to homes now. No apparent evidence she's a vampire (or Campire) beyond that.

Bridget: We left her at home over Thankgiving break by accident. Mom felt terrible but she was fine. Weirdly good at taking care of herself, which is good because I just heard Harry and Mom come in and she got left at the dentist.

Gotta go. Learning to tie this ascot.

[Alexa Garcia]

A breakthrough in psychic powers!

So, for a long time now I haven't been able to do anything in Introduction to the Mind. I told you about that right, stranger journal?

The teacher, Mrs. Jarvo, told me I was blocking my abilities too much by worrying. But worrying is what I do! So, she would sit there with her exploded head of pink hair and say in her squeaky voice that I needed to lighten up, like she didn't sound like a cartoon character. Mr. Jarvo probably gets in trouble for laughing. Probably.

Anyway, I guess she was right because I never was able to read someone until today. What happened was, we were doing our normal exercises where we pair off and practice sort of imagining a page of

The Dance

something—a picture or a word or whatever—and then the other person reads it. I guess being really close to the other person helps because the connection is shorter.

So, I was sitting across from Louis, who is in Students for Safety and is really strong as a psychic, so he saw what I was doing immediately (a picture of my grandma's dog Beatriz, rendered with crosshatch shading). And then it was my turn. I said I wasn't very good, and Louis wasn't having any of it. He just said to relax and do it. I sat back and closed my eyes and took a deep breath and as I let the breath out something white and rectangular appeared!

I took another breath and when I let this one out, the white blur turned into a piece of paper. It said, "Hi Alexa, will you go to the dance with me? Louis."

Uh, right! Okay. Well, I mean he's pretty handsome or something? But I didn't say anything. I was just like, "Yay, I saw a paper." Because I did!

[Phoebe Case]

It's been a solid ten years since I've been this excited about going to a high school dance. In part because I am twenty-seven and that is when I was actually in high school.

Yes, I was seventeen and it was homecoming at Neptune High, where I was a student. And I *needed* to go to that dance. I had the eye of Boscoe Tran who was the most exciting guy at the school. He asked me out by unveiling a cleverly folded banner on top of my VW Bug in the VIP parking lot. How could I say no? I was in love.

Boscoe *was* cool. He had gauges, and he was born into a Filipino street bike racing gang where he rose through the ranks to lieutenant by the age of ten. I once heard he jump kicked a vice principal in the neck! Every time I saw his spiky mohawk my knees got wobbly. I knew then I had to really impress him and worked all night on a note I handed him.

It didn't work out, but that wasn't Boscoe's fault.

[Alexa Garcia] [private journal]

Truth time: I tried to back out of the dance, but Monika insisted. And I couldn't say no to that one. Now we are going thrift store dress shopping. No escape for me.

I don't think I said anything on here about what happened with Monika after I saw her go through my back yard to go to the Matrix (the Internet). After she got rescued from the Matrix by Damien I stopped by the medical center to give her a cupcake. Grandma had us making cupcakes for a church social on Sunday and there were tons of extras.

And honestly, I felt guilty, because I saw her sneaking by when she was going into the Matrix and didn't even say hello or try to help or say that she didn't need to do anything.

So, I told her all that in a big, rambling speech and she said, "Tak," which is "thank you" in Danish. And ever since we have been closer, I think. We stop to talk in the hallways of the 200 building between classes every day. And she has a different lunch than me but sometimes she sneaks into mine.

She is from Kobnhavn, which is like the only big city in Denmark. She is here because she is staying with a foster family while her mom is trapped inside a video game. We're so similar! And she has a very good sense of humor that is very dry.

It's really nice, I will have to be careful.

The Dance

[Alexa Garcia]

Okay, so I have an idea, Louis. I will go to the dance with you, but why don't we all just go as a group? I don't have a date or anything. I just want to, like, do the dance, and have fun and leave. Okay? Let's do that!

    Monika and Mikey are still going. It's gonna be a whole group!

[MAX Rushmore]

The dance is tonight.
    I'm gonna puke.

[Juan Addams]

What would Dill Cross do? What would Udiak Gonzales do? What would Seluvion the nine-thousand-year-old high school senior do?

[Halvo O]

We gather at the Olive Garden, shepherded by parents in eights and tens. Done up to the nines.
    I have spilled marinara on my jacket. Oh, no.

[GOMEZ]

Halvo! Retreat to the back restroom on the left. I teleported you wetnaps and a breath mint.

[Natalie Lavigne]

This evening, as I was getting out my dance stuff, I went to my window because there was a loud knocking. This was strange because windows do not knock, they usually tap or rap. But it was knocking like on a solid wood door.

I pulled up the blinds and on the windowsill was a huge black bird. Not sure of the etymology. Four wings, so not a crow? It spoke in a deep man voice, like what a manager has. It said, "Complete the January reading assignment early, or you will pay dearly."

So, I'm reading now and very intently, and I can't go to the dance. Sorry everyone.

[Cole Abrams]

So, I guess you forgot you said you would go to the dance with me?

Nah, it's fine. Don't worry about it. I'll just head there on my own. No hard feelings.

I mean, the SFS will be there and Mrs. Konrath and a ton of other people I know. We go to the same school with a lot of people. Maybe I'll even see JR And nod at him approvingly. As opposed to not approvingly.

And Nat, you're welcome to join if you get it done. I know you're a fast reader.

Disturbingly fast, actually.

[Natalie Lavigne]

The bird is back.

This time when it knocked on the window (does it have something that produces a wood-door knock?) it asked me what I had written on page four of my reading assignment's report. That's exactly how it was worded: my reading assignment's report.

So. Sir. I think I'm not quite off the hook.

[Cole Abrams]

It's fine, Nat. Just stay home. That's weird. You don't need to keep giving excuses.

Stop trying to make it okay, though. You said you would go. I got new clothes and I wasn't even going to.

The Dance

[Natalie Lavigne]

Sir,

Um, so the bird is back, and it said in its man voice, "Your report is accepted. You will receive your grade from your human teacher in time."

I hadn't even turned it in, but it was done in my bag.

I'm rushing to get ready, so if you're up for it still, come get me? I promise I'll be done and ready at seven.

[Cole Abrams]

One time a kid from a rival dojo cornered me in an alley in his dad's car. Also, in his dad's car? Four of his toughest friends.

Another time a bad wizard tried to trap me in a book. A Class IV shadow tome.

And let's not forget the time Louis fell into that 4-D Hypercube nest over on Fountain and I got him out basically just with punching.

I've handled it all, so can you please explain to me why I am sitting on the curb in front of this girl's house an hour after she promised she would be ready? I can't even see anything in the windows. It's just dark and there's nothing.

She said she would be here. Again. This always happens. Why am I such an idiot?

[Cole Abrams]

I will never forgive you for this, Nat! You are incorrigible!

NAT
Did you just use the word incorrigible?

COLE
Yes

Well, it suits you, sir.

Thanks.

So...are you going to the dance

I am. Maybe I will see you there? I would like that.

Okay.

WAIT! NO! I'm outside your house right now! Why aren't you ready? Where are you?

I can't even.

[GOMEZ]

An unexpected connection is the spice of life, particularly when it comes to social events. While there are many skilled tango dancers at the school (and that is surprising), I did not expect Ebit Nicole (of morning announcements and choir fame) to be such a darned superior partner. I spun her like a top, and it was satisfying in a way I'm not sure I can put into words.

[Oliver 181]

I want to formally apologize for flying over the dance floor and buzzing the DJ booth in protest of the song choices.

[Cole Abrams]

Screw this. Okay, I'm heading over. Let's tear the gym up!

The Dance

[Kelli Konrath, CEED]

If I see another student post on here during the actual dance I'm going to give you detention. Stop wasting your youth posting. I mean it. I'm going to kick you, Cole.

[Phoebe Case]

I definitely just saw Natalie and her muscley ex-partner in the halls outside the gym and they were SMOOCHING!

You can't deny it. I saw the little electrical arcs jumping between them and zapping the lockers behind them. It would be a simple thing to get paint flecks off of those lockers (1102-1116 should do it) and test for energy smooch residue using one of the carbon dating kits from the laboratory.

[JR Benton]

Excuse me, I happen to make out in front of 1110 three or four times a week. With Camila Flay. Who really enjoys it like I do. You'll find all sorts of big romance energy aaaaall over that section of lockers.

[Disapproving Narwhal]

Gross.

[Pleeb Ymambo]

Yuck!

[Hyper Akeelah]

JR, stop.

[Camila Flay]

I saw the post by JR, and can I just say: no. He and I do not make out in front of 1110. In fact, seniors will remember 1112 was the site of the epic breakup between Esmerelda and Marshall Kuwai, and it is reportedly still very uncomfortable to kiss there.

Also, I am still inside the Maw.

JR, you are such a goon! But I will forgive you on one condition. Bring me Magpies soft serve by fifth period on Monday. Velvet cake non-dairy with butterfinger bits. I don't know how to get it inside the Maw but figure it out.

Your life hangs in the balance.

[Phoebe Case]

Wait, but if JR was lying, then that means that the high incidence of energy smooch residue means…

Sorry I just dropped my phone. I don't have a revelation. If it wasn't the SFS lovebirds or that guy, I don't know what's going on.

Also has anyone seen my purse? I left it on a chair at the mermaid table.

[DOCTOR M]

Daily step count: 49,981

The Dance

[Alexa Garcia]

The dance was so fun! At least, for a while.

[Monika M]

I think the dance was swell!

 I have been coming here two years and Winterween is my favorite and always will be. The gym is decorated with actual Cursed Forest decorations as an homage to the famous trek through the Blue Underbrush where the woods tried to stop them from delivering presents to the newborn King of Winter. And St. Nick is there, also. It's Drew the Janitor dressed up in a bad mall Santa outfit. He is too skinny to be in the outfit so he looks very much like he should be eating more.

 And there's a snowfall but it's magic so it isn't cold. It just sets the mood. It is a very fun atmosphere and there is a DJ and a live band both and we danced a lot and I feel bad for other schools where a dance is a terrifying negotiation. Just cut loose! Even Alexa, who is a little awkward in her skin (I love you, Alexa!), danced with me for hours and was having so much fun. At least, she was for a while, but then I guess the evening caught up with her because I didn't see her leave.

 I was even surprised because Micah came to visit (!) from Denmark. He showed up in dramatic fashion by appearing in a cloud of snow that burst out of the ground as the clock struck 22:22. The combined wishes of the student body must have allowed it to happen. I don't think Micah was expecting it because he was in shorts and a bathrobe. Still, when he saw me he came up and set a very good kiss on my face and there was polite applause from everyone around us.

 So, all in all, it was a really fun dance and I'm glad I go here. I wish they let you come back after you graduate but it is explicitly stated at the start of the dance that if you have graduated you are not allowed (except faculty chaperones).

Paranormal School 13

[Alexa Garcia]

I left the dance the way you're supposed to according to movies. I saw something upsetting and then said everything was fine and then ran out the doors and down steps. I actually started laughing partway down the steps into the neighborhood because I realized what I was doing, but the laugh felt weird and bad, like it sort of hurt. You know the laugh you make when someone is picking on you, and you say it isn't a big deal and you laugh but it comes out all high and weird? It was one of those.

So, you all already know this, but during one of the songs, I maybe used my powers and projected a bunch of stuff up into the air in the gym for Monika. It was mostly fine but as my mind wandered a bunch of weird stuff appeared, like the bra I was wearing before I changed into the dress…

And then there was Monika, running across my yard and me just standing there watching and not doing anything.

You know how when you remember something, and then see a video of the same thing, they look different? Well, this backyard moment looked different than I remembered it. Monika was there a long time, and I was very close by. In the little floating projection, you could practically reach out and touch her with one hand, and the other could get to me.

And I looked over, and sure enough, there she was, watching the little scene, and when she looked at me, she looked so surprised. So, I left.

All things considered, it could have been worse. Maybe she will still want to be friends. After all, this time it wasn't so much a secret about her as one about me.

Even at a surreal dance decorated with magical snow and trees that sway inside a gym, you must remember that people are just people, and we don't know what we're doing. Especially me. Sorry for ruining the evening, everyone.

The Dance

[Mikey12]

If we're apologizing I also want to say sorry for ruining the evening. I promise I will learn how to fix walls and patch that hole up. Werewolf antics!

[Cole Abrams]

When I left the dance, I was honestly in pretty good spirits. It was a lot of fun, and I made unexpected friends with a bunch of theatre students and one of the wood dolls, who is honestly really funny. The kind of evening I could see thinking back to in adulthood with the wisdom of hindsight and say, "Honestly, that was better than just going with Nat as my date like I expected to."

But on the walk home, as the music faded and I was left to my own thoughts, I pictured myself jumping up and hurrying over to Nat's place even though she'd just… constantly not done a single thing she said she would. But that one little glimmer of us maybe still going to the dance and it being a <u>thing</u> and it was like I was mind-controlled. Like I was puppeted by an arcane Ki-artist.

Hah.

So, I got home, and I was pretty angry. I may have thrown the ascot in the recycling.

[Natalie Lavigne] [secret diary]

Millie,

When it was late, and I was sure the parents were asleep, I did something I shouldn't have. But I felt like I had to. You understand, don't you, Millie? I had to make things right.

And so, I came down the stairs and sat on the last one in the dark. And golden tendrils etched in space and opened a portal that quietly hummed and lit the room in a faint warm glow. My stomach was very displeased. I'd never done something like this and I was supposed to save this sort of mischief for later. But...

Cole was there. I was looking down on him as his head lay on his pillow. The angle gave his high cheekbones a certain prominence. I wanted to giggle, but also, he was right there and I didn't want to disturb him.

His eyes focused and he looked up at me. And I may have kissed him. Just once, but I meant it, Millie.

And it was time to close the portal and return to bed.

I wonder how my counterpart felt about it. I shall ask him when the time is right.

The Dance

[Phoebe Case]

My lava lamp's wax has been hardened on a glob for a while now, but I just looked over as I was getting ready for bed after the dance and lo, it was *melted*. This is a sign.

Someone somewhere had some romance!

Makes my heart all aflutter.

I may have received some questions from my peers here about my time at high school in the 2000s. Specifically, how I was both home-schooled and a high schooler. The truth is, my mother finally broke and enrolled me in time for my freshman year.

Ah, freshman year. I almost forgot. I was out to catch the eye of Tim Short, the son of Principal Short. Tim was <u>not</u> short, that's for sure. Standing next to him was like standing next to a palm tree. (He also had a big head.)

Alas, it wasn't meant to be. But the dance was fun! Just like this one.

Good night, Edendale High School11!

[BIRD]

Necessary tasks are accomplished in a growing cascade, like the warm wind beneath feathered arms, pushing us up. To a better tomorrow.

I fly for the stars.

Screeeeee!

[Annabelle Yes]

Did any of you know diners never close? I know some do. I'm talking about the other ones, like Astro. You can go there with friends <u>at any time</u> and sit and eat pancakes and talk to them. Why have you been keeping this from me??

    I just turned in a report on splines, and a book report on *The Moon* by Dill Cross, and my group delivered their big student government presentation in Ant Control, and just needed to chill out, y'know? And Bandido's was closed because it was midnight.

    But you know what isn't closed?
    DINERS.

[Annabelle Yes]

I am hearing IRL that people knew about the diners for years on account of their group activities. Good for you! Congratulations on socializing. What's your GPA, huh?

[Natalie Lavigne] [secret diary]

Dearest, dearest Millie,

I had a long conversation with my dad last night!

He usually doesn't get home until very late, and that's if he's in town. And when he is in town and is home late the best I can hope for is a late-night chat where he drifts to sleep on the couch, and I race tired, falling eyelids to get across my day as quickly as possible.

At first he says he is resting his eyes. Then he says he is just resting his head, and I can tell when I am done because the whiskers in his beard start shaking as his sleepy breaths kick in.

It sounds kinda sad when I write it out, but I really like it. He's a good listener.

But tonight! Tonight, he was already home when I got home. It was crazy. Like, really really crazy. I made a little squeaky noise when I saw him. He was making dinner. Dough was out for dumplings, and all the veggies and meats and stuff were in little identically sized piles, like only he can do. The Hanukah playlist warbled off the TV. It'd already given up and started on Christmas songs, so he must have been home for a while.

The first words out of my mouth were, "Who are you and what have you done with my father?"

And he laughed, which is good, because I was maybe just a little ready to hit the distress call button on my wristband. Get that on-alert SFS team to me pronto.

But yeah, he was home early because his trip had been cut short. I hung out in the kitchen while he finished dinner, and we chatted about all kinds of things. School, my work at

SFS, the Skullhunters saga. He loved hearing about that because he was also involved in foiling apocalyptic pranks in his high school days.

And then the conversation drifted to Cole. And he was so excited to hear about my ex-partner and I had to confess about what happened. With the SFS teams and the dance. And I might have left some details out, but I did mention a face interaction.

And Dad said, "Well, why don't you have him over for dinner? I want to meet him."

But I haven't talked to Cole since the dance.

And I didn't expect this but for some reason, I got really sad when I said that, and I could feel tears well up in my eyes. I tried to keep it together, but you don't fool a dad, especially one fully conscious and pressing dumpling sides together with the back of a fork.

Dad did the Dad thing and crumpled up a napkin and threw it at me. And he said, "It'll be okay, Dolly," which is what he used to say to me when I was five.

After dinner, I messaged Cole, but he hasn't written back.

Am I terrible person? I might be a terrible person. Surely he understands. Right?

God's Day Off
by Alexa
(I was fourteen when I wrote this)

They say that when your kid has a kid, you're done being a parent.
So, I hear.

For a moment
A pause
A work break
In the break room
With laminate tables and plastic chairs
With daytime miasma on the TV
Hocking wares and arguments

So, I imagine the big guy
(Lady?)
(Indeterminate omnipotent entity?)
Sitting next to half-day-old coffee
In a clear carafe
Watching me up on the TV
Wrapped up tight in flannel

Watching my brother
Tear open the box to the game I bought him
Slam that disc into his PlayStation
Oblivious to the humans around
Until brunch beckons

"This is what it's all about,"
s/he might say.

God's Day Off

SPRING SEMESTER

[Alexa Garcia] [private journal]

It's light out but the sun is farther away so it's orange and sideways. My window at home faces east and in the winter I get the sun first, around the time my neighbor's rooster flips out.

I'm always out of bed fast, even if I don't feel like it, because otherwise I won't get a chance to take a shower.

My little brother is at the old beige computer in the kitchen. Looks like he's finishing a report at the last minute. He looks like he's been up for hours scrambling. I wish I had his discipline: play for weeks and then panic and rush at the end.

> *A rushing rabbit*
> *hops when he must,*
> *plays otherwise.*
> *It's purity*
> *that darts.*

Homework is always a steady marathon for me. One lap at a time.

The shower is the bathtub kind and when it is cold outside (I know it doesn't get THAT cold here, shh), the water takes forever to warm up. So, I stand there wrapped up in the faded pink bathrobe I inherited from Grandma. My bed was warm. The bathrobe is warm. Everywhere else is cold—even the shower sometimes.

Sometimes, I'll catch my own eye in the mirror. When I see myself I'm always embarrassed, like I'm checking in with a friend and I want to say, "Yeah, I know. Leave me alone."

The shower's spray is too narrow. One time when I was still at normal high school, we went on a class trip in track and stayed in a hotel down in San Diego. The hotel shower was like a wall of hot water. I never wanted to leave.

Was this what it was like in the womb? Safe. For now.

I walk down the hill as the sun hits the layers of houses in the hills opposite and reflects orange off their windows. Even now it feels a little less cold than it was.

Sunset is already busy with cars. They hang bumpers-out into the intersection, and I have to weave around drivers to get through the crosswalk. The little bakery is open, and I can smell coffee and bread when I walk by. It's been around since I was a little kid, but now instead of a chalkboard menu they have a big TV screen. A football (soccer) match is on. I don't follow the guy leagues. Maybe European teams are playing?

By the way, is it true that the US Women's National Team has a witch on it? Not like a pointy hat broom witch, just heard a rumor a certain player is descended from a long line. This is what comes up at lunch now.

The opposite neighborhood has steep streets and I trudge up the one the school is on. It's there like it always is, with that little humble Edendale High School sign. The fake sign says the "Pumpkin Collective" is on Thursday at seven p.m. I've never been to a Pumpkin Collective. What is that? Do you go to a pumpkin patch? Does the pumpkin patch have any doors floating in space or weird vortexes? Is the farmer a winged skeleton dragon?

On the other side of the fence, the actual PS13 yard is strangely calm. The only truly strange thing I can make out today is that Monika is sitting with the wooden mannequin clique. I'll hear about it in first period.

Or maybe I won't. Maybe this is it and I screwed up and she's found new friends who are more interesting than me. I don't really believe the wood people are more interesting than me, but they're popular for a reason I haven't figured out yet. So that's what I tell myself as Monika waves me over.

The bell rings.

[Ebit Nicole]

TRANSCRIPT OF MORNING ANNOUNCEMENTS FOR MONDAY, JANUARY 9

Good morning PS13! This is Ebit Nicole and Don Chang. And this is the first day of a brand-new school semester!

The weather today is sunny and brisk. Temperature will be fifty-nine degrees.

This day in Paranormal School System history: We say hello and "thanks for best wishes" from Paranormal School 7, from its home high up on the edge of the Eritrean Highlands in Asmara! We'll do our best to learn. You too, PS7!

Lunch today is huge tamales. Due to an ordering error, you will have to "teamala" up with your bestie or bae to take on these team-sized tamales. Special double-wide lunch trays will be provided. This may be a problem for Don, who does not share.

One small announcement: the Chess Boyz club will be renamed to Chess Men.

If Ebit Nicole had her way, she might talk for up to forty minutes about visiting the PS7 campus, its art-deco design, Eritrean street food, and any number of other unsolicited details about our beloved sister campus and its city. Since she is overruled…

That is all. Have a safe, productive day, Paranormal School!

[Alexa Garcia]

A new year is here! My New Year's Resolution is simple. I want to focus on my work here. My grades have been okay, but I know I can do better. This is a magnet school, after all. Time to be a magnet school student!

[Annabelle Yes]

Class selection as a senior is so weird. They know we're all special because we wouldn't be at PS13 if we weren't a bunch of supernaturally abled weirdos, but do they have to be so pessimistic about our odds of landing normal jobs?

I went in and the first thing out of the instructor's mouth was about how I should consider counterespionage or something. I said I wanted to be a nurse, and he gave me a look like I was grade-A crazy. Popular normie fiction franchises paint a picture that witches and wizards grow up to become cops and bus drivers. I guess not.

Surely there's some kind of 500 class that fits that. I'm supposed to have a counselor meeting with my mom tomorrow night. I'm going to raise some serious hell!

Also, Natalie, don't be late for our portal practice sesh.

[Mikey12]

It's a whole new year and a whole new Mikey. And by new, I mean old. I'm still wolfed out. Dad says it's fine, but he had to install special new doors and I shredded three scratching stumps over the holiday break. The building supply store apparently is asking him questions, and my dad isn't the best with confrontation.

I am, though! I am a seven-foot-tall pro wrestler covered in fur. Damien let me throw him like a javelin on New Year's Eve. Aside from him, not many people have come to hang out, but that's fine. I get it. I am a giant monster.

[Natalie Lavigne]

As the slipstream folds are getting more precise and stable, I'm starting to notice more stuff in the null space "between" the two places than I used to. I know some of it is wireless radio signals, but there're also sometimes familiar-feeling golden tendrils that show time and causality. The end destination of a bike messenger. Snakes behind a van driver, connected to the back of their neck, leading all the way back to the rental place parking lots. The location of a pair of pants' lost button.

And my favorite—little notes left by something to *something else* in this other space. Sneaky sneaky.

Now that I type it all out, I can see why people find this stuff unnerving. I get it! It doesn't help that there are very few dimensional adepts around. And the ones I do know of are… not my speed. Remind me to tell you about the last Vector Apocryphant who came to dinner.

[Phoebe Case]

A new year! You know what that means? Time to update the ol' style for the new semester.

It's true, the cool rebellious kids have disbanded and now I'm the only one left at the bleachers during lunch and after school. Is there no one left that both wants to stick it to the man but also look extremely "fire"?

Oh, in less cool news, I have decided the extensive research I have conducted here will be collected in a new volume. That's right. Phoebe is branching out. We're doing a book! Tell Cameron Crowe thanks for the idea.

If I'm being honest, I got a little distracted in my days hanging at the bench with Kyle, Lance, Teemo, and all the rest. I may not have done many interviews or even opened the notes app on my phone since, uh… it's not important. But the real-world calls and Phoebe is on the Case!

By the way, don't go to crackedcase.website, I guess I also didn't check my work email for a while and the hosting ran out. And someone bought it.

Why is all this stuff so hard?

[Mayumi Ikazaki]

Hi.

I'm Mayumi Ikazaki. This is my mandatory journal. No, I never wrote the pinned introduction post you're supposed to do. But I have to if I want to graduate. Which seems wrong. I'm a senior. I have seniority. I am

above

this.

Who am I? I just transferred here. I was once captain of the rugby team. No, I don't have any powers. I was let into the school because of some obscure rule. No, I don't have some latent psychic ability or super strength. I am just fast and tough.

That's enough. Normalize Not Caring. Ciaoooo.

[Cole Abrams] [personal log]

What a weird way to start off the year.

I just got back from Nat's house. After the dance (and that surprise upside-down portal-enabled kiss), I don't hear from her until yesterday.

And she invited me over. Like she does. But somehow this time she was actually home. And it wasn't just her.

Her house is way up on the hill overlooking the reservoir. It's this tall, thin gray house with those glass blocks like they had everywhere in the 1980s.

Her mom answered the door. I guess she was in town. She's one of those white ladies with a brushstroke of gray hair and the round glasses who is always near a plant. She introduced herself and didn't seem to know who I was, but we hit it off fast while we waited for Nat to come downstairs. I told her I was reading Dill Cross's book about the Depths of Veromang, and I think she was surprised by that. Despite the title, it's pretty academic.

Nat comes down and steps outside with me and we sit on the red brick steps to the porch for a while and talk about SFS business. What JR is being suspended for now, what I've been doing around a missing stack of forbidden scrolls from the library, what Nat might do as a SFS project since she isn't "on patrol" anymore. That leads to talk of Quimby's comic and what the cryptic jokes the cat makes actually might mean.

And she makes a comment about my new jacket (lucky break—a mom Target purchase that I really like) and about how it suits my personality and I'm just... I'm on board in spite of everything. And she is wearing this super cute little shirt thing that's like a sun dress except without the skirt part, and she smells not so faintly like flowers and sunscreen.

And I know I'm skipping over a lot but then we kissed again.

Okay, so, kissing Nat is like...

I'm going to try to explain.

I do not kiss a lot of girls. There was Olivia on a dare in seventh grade. There was my ex-girlfriend Jasmine. And Morgana, who doesn't count (she was an evil sorceress, and we were in her lair/the photography darkroom). My sample size of girls is small, but I think I've had good luck with kissing. Good kisses. Long kisses. Short kisses.

But Natalie. I don't understand. I didn't think kisses could be so soft. It was like little tiptoes on air. How does someone who can punch that hard be so gentle? Brother, it's confusing.

Ah whatever. She's the best kisser I am aware of. Maybe the best in Los Angeles County.

[Mikey12]

One of my new classes for the semester is just called "The Unknowable." I've never heard of it, and no one can tell me anything about it except that it happens during third period in room 581. According to my little paper with my classes on it. Hard not to shred it on my huge werewolf claws. Gentle!

I've never even been in the 500 building. It's always there next to the student parking lot, three boxy beige mid-80s brick stories of mystery. When I peer into the windows, I see into my own soul, rather than the soul of the classroom, um, contents.

(I know it's my soul because there's a lot of wolf stuff in there. Moon, trees, cool looking wolf faces)

It's hard to get into and out of the doorways to the various buildings. I have to take my little backpack off and cinch in sideways.

[Damien Cross]

I've got the Unknowable class, too.

Mikey is a freshman. Why would I have a freshman class?

I haven't talked to that guy much after the Matrix incident. He got kinda weird TBH, not talking about the werewolf part. Also, there was an incident over holiday break with pirates, competing treasure hunter groups, and a certain lost treasure (gold beetle with ruby eyes).

That beetle could talk, so it is staying with me while it gets back on its feet.

I'm gonna go try to get into this building for this mystery class.

[Rodney Gemini (Moon Facet)]

Fam, how do you get into the 500 building? I'm going to be late for this mystery class. I tried the main doors but when I opened them and walked through, I was walking right back out onto the landing in front of the steps.

I keep trying. I can see the hallway inside. I can see people moving around in it! When I yell they beckon to me but when I walk through the doorway I'm facing back the other way. It's like the cars in the parking lot are mocking me.

I am smarter than a car! Shut up!

[Cole Abrams]

Fair warning, I've been quiet since the start of the year because I've been trying to figure out the Unknowable class. I got the assignment, too. It's weird that the class is assigned to people from multiple grade levels at once, but it's hardly the weirdest thing at the school. That remains the broom closet in the restricted wing of the library.

[Cole Abrams]

I got to the first class.

[Xenton X]

Cole, don't hold out on us. How did you get to the class? Did we miss it? Can we make it up? Is this going to wreck my pristine GPA?
Cole!
COLE!!!

An Internship

[Mikey12]

Last night I had a nightmare. It was scary because I could see the future. We were the last survivors of an alien invasion of Los Angeles. They'd sent the marines and it didn't go well. They'd sent the army and it didn't go well. They sent a ragtag guerrilla squad made up of past and present players of the LA Kings and it really didn't go well.

So, we were left to our own devices, up in the hills behind Griffith Park. Alien groundships were slithering in from all sides and bursting up from the ground to grab randoms. One of those classic nightmares everyone has where the last thing that happens is living steel cables wrap around your bod and a little face with big jet-black alien eyes say, "We have you now, Mikey12."

When I woke up, I saw I'd smashed my bed frame apart. And I did what I always do when I am scared and hopped on Vulcan to shop for today's super crazy discount. I really love Vulcan not only for its sleek shopping experience, but for how comforting stuff can be. Mostly I use it to buy stuff I use, like XXXXL t-shirts or a wrist band that vibrates when you are close to a Starbucks. One time, I bought a duvet and my dad uses it in the AirBnB room. I guess I'm a little young to be using Vulcan, and I might be putting too many things on my credit card, but

An Internship

maybe I'm just mature for my age. Certainly, I think I've grown a lot this year.

I'm not referring to the werewolf transformation, I mean inside. Mikey13 stuff!

[Ms. Cartwright, Teacher]

Thanks to the off-brand audio/video recording device that was last week's deal on Vulcan, I have acquired multiple students' secret passwords to disable their cheating spells (and probably some other nefarious secrets, since one compromised student was infamous provocateur JR Benton). Now we will have an honest assessment of how well you know George Orwell's *1984*.

Prepare yourselves, students!

[ANDERTON NEO]

Hello Paranormal School students and faculty!

My name is Anderton Neo. You certainly know that name and this face. But what you don't know is it is not the name I was born with. I'm an alumnus from the PS13 class of 2002 and I created my new P-Name (paranormal name) at the very school I am visiting today!

I'm here representing Vulcan, the company I created in my parents' unused office building after graduating from PS13. Our app is probably on all of your phones right now, right? It's more for adults, but you're welcome to "get browsing!"

If you are unable to use a smartphone due to an electromagnetic condition, Vulcan uses all kinds of data and good old fashioned "intuition" to recommend things to buy and do that are uniquely, perfectly suited to you! It's really, really cool when it works—and it mostly does! You might be feeling a little let down because a vegan pizza party you had been 'cooking up' fell through, or your birthday party only has a dozen confirmations. No big deal, right? Especially if what's really going on is you need a new safety razor. I know. It doesn't make any sense, but it works!

Or I should say, it works well enough. For now. But it will be picked down to the skeleton by competitors in time. We must innovate!

I know some of you are looking at going into tech after you graduate, and I wanted to help my fellow tech-paras "get with it." I'll have some folks at the school this afternoon after sixth period so you can come by check out a number of choice internships we have starting next week. And if you can't right now, we'll have something going this summer, too. Bring a resume and a great attitude, and I know we'll have a place for you at Vulcan.

And hey! Maybe if you're *really* cool, you'll get to see the *really* cool thing we're doing next! A glimpse of the future. ;)

-Anderton Neo-
-Get Browsing-
-Vulcan-

[ANDERTON NEO]

The turnout for the internships was amazing! Thank you all who came out. These are some great-looking resumes. Really proud to be an alum.

We have great big plans, and we need your help, interns! Please show up to the former American Apparel factory on Sunset on your start day, grab a smock and a snack bar keycode from security, and get ready to Change the World! More soon! Seriously, we're going to blow the roof off the planet in a week.

-Anderton Neo-
-Get Browsing-
-Vulcan-

An Internship

[Ebit Nicole]

TRANSCRIPT OF MORNING ANNOUNCEMENTS FOR TUESDAY, FEBRUARY 7

Good morning PS13! This is Ebit Nicole. Don Chang has refused to do the morning announcements ever again.

The weather today is overcast. High is sixty-six degrees. Not bad.

This day in Paranormal School System history: Did you know springtime is the perfect time to befriend the fae? Take a guided hike with Torreflot into the Angeles National Forrest and to the mysterious Magical Mines where refugees from the Depths of Veromang have set up shop. Pick up a slice of pizza made from their charmed oven and dangle your legs over the void in the sonic and literal glow of a mushroom choir from another realm. "Realm" is another word for dimension.

Don would never have the guts to check out something so wondrous, but you could!

Lunch today is grilled cheese.

That is all. Have a safe, cushy day, Paranormal School! Make sure you don't tell anyone how you really feel, so that you can be mad at them for no reason later!

[Alexa Garcia]

I got in.

!!!!!!!!!

I get to do work study intern things at Vulcan and leave school early one day a week until the end of the school year. I wish it was more days off, but I'll take what I can get.

It's at Vulcan, the tech company that opened up a new office in the desecrated husk of that American Apparel factory. Transparent leotard looms have given way to transparent cubicle walls and super soft bean bag chairs set into semicircles and lots of neck scarves for some reason. Someone said a vast comedy theater was gonna move into this spot, but I'm glad it was a tech company instead. I know a couple of people at the improv club and they're the worst!

JK, love you, Juan!

Okay, so wait. I'm getting off topic. I didn't even say what the best part was. They have a machine that does what I do! I got to see it and they're announcing some huge thing with it tonight. The last time Anderton Neo made an announcement like this they put out Vulcan. I've seen the YouTube of it. People were screaming their heads off.

Holy cow holy cow holy cow.

[ANDERTON NEO]

It's gone time. If I could wink in text form, I would.

Oh, right. I can.

;)

-Anderton Neo-
-XXXXXXXX-
-XXXX XXXX-

An Internship

[Sam Mitchmoon]

I can't sleep. It's five a.m. and when is Anderton going to announce the airships?

That's what he's going to do right? Announce the airships he promised for this year?

[ANDERTON NEO]

I was joking about the announcement! And if everyone could please just delete and reinstall their Vulcan app, you'll find it has a new logo! That is the news I was really hinting at. Hence the joke! Who would create hype about a world-shattering new app from Vulcan, even at a tiny scale on an ancient java website designed by some moron in 1998? Not me!

I love you all. The world changes forever, irreversibly, in the near future!

-Anderton Neo-
-Get Browsing-
-Vulcan-

[Damien Cross]

I was outvoted and Mikey the Wolf, Phoebe, Sven, and JR made me go to the Bandido coffee place. I must have been there for an hour before I realized there was no purpose to this. It wasn't a redux Question Society. There were no plans to go into an alternate dimension or secured psychic danger zone. I was so confused.

We just... sat there. Talking. And drinking cold coffee with butterscotch flavor in it.

Also, the old guy that runs the place is pretty nice, I guess. We talked a while.

[Adult Lyle]

Oh hey, Damien! It was super neat hanging out with you and your friend the other day. Glad you guys came through Bandido's. It's weird how early it gets dark right now, huh?

You know who you remind me of? Verity Claswell. She was—and sorry cause I know you're not a lady but hear me out!—she was the best rock climber in college, and she also did those super long distance trail runs. I thought she was super tough and cool, but the thing that I think you both have in common is you're really curious. You see the world and you can't *not* find things. That was the real nuts part about Verity. She would find a hidden trail or some outcrop during her normal climb and would explore it and then just come back and win the race! Blew my mind.

She was also a babe, but again, we are talking about the curiosity part.

Anyway, so maybe it's okay to have friends and to also do your thing is my point. You don't have to do everything with them, and you don't have to join every club they start just to be friends.

Stop by any time you want a cold brew and a chat, man!

Also, I'm forty-one. Not exactly old. Gray hairs come for us all, li'l dude!

[Damien Cross]

Huh, thanks. I hadn't thought about it that way. Thanks.

Huh.

Bus

[Annabelle Yes]

I saved someone today. I was outside at the bus circle right after school let out, heading to my ride. There was this little pale dapper guy, the one with the slicked back black hair and widows peak, he got on the Moonside Bus without paying attention to where he was going, and the doors slid shut and he panicked.

Is that bus super dangerous? Certainly, that's the rumor. It doesn't obey the laws of physics. I mean, the students that ride it seem okay. It's merely in the top twenty most dangerous parts of the PS13 campus.

Pleeb Ymambo rides the Moonside, and they wear the same clothes every day and their hair are always the same. That's weird but not necessarily dangerous.

So, the li'l guy seemed freaked out enough and they were banging on the windows and stuff, so before the bus ceased to be in the bus circle, I slipped open a slipstream fold into the bus and pulled him through by the loop on his backpack. He said thanks a million, planted a kiss on the back of my hand, and marched off.

When I looked back at the bus circle, the Moonside Bus had gone.

I guess my ability did some good today, didn't it?

[Annabelle Yes]

I'm at home. My ride just dropped me off. I'm still thinking about that moon bus. And saving people, I guess. Mentoring has been my favorite part of this last year. Nat and the others work hard and are so excited. I know they'll be great.

But maybe I can do other things to help people? I've already volunteered to get it onto my college applications. That was fun and definitely worth it, but we are discouraged from using our abilities out in the normal world and there're only so many shelter dogs I can walk in an afternoon. I guess I could just flip open a portal, dump a trio of dogs into their cages, and grab more mid-walk, but depending on the neighborhood someone might say something.

Paranormal and federal agencies have special liaisons to Paranormal School, but they don't like visiting, and they really don't like talking to ordinary cops after an "incident" out in the city.

"Oh, that coyote turned into a person on Benton that people were screaming about. Well, there's this secret school within a school in Echo Park and that was probably one of the students."

[Vert Merpson]

Annabelle, I know what you mean about the powers stuff. But how do you know so much about the liaisons from the police? I only knew we had that detective liaison because he talked to my class because someone had been getting stray cats and running them up and down neighborhood streets in delta formations. Just a wing of thirty cats.

He seemed more tired than mad.

[Annabelle Yes]

I know because I interviewed Detective Johnson for my college applications. It helps to have some important people on there for references and being curious about someone is a great way to make them like you.

When he heard I could use runic arts to open slipstream portals, he got super interested and asked if I would open one to his ex-wife's document safe, but I said no.

·–·

[Natalie Lavigne]

Miss,

I will be late to our lunch meeting I think. We are dealing with something at SFS. All hands call went out on the wristbands.

Save some cultured discussion for me.

[Annabelle Yes]

Nat, that's fine. You're keeping the school safe. I might be your mentor, but there's plenty you can do I can't. Go do your stuff.

Speaking of safety, does anyone have any info about the Moonside Bus? I tried to open a fold to where it normally sits in the bus circle, but all that was there was a dark cave-looking space with aurora borealis stuff around it. First time I tried opening a portal and got something that looked like it was out of a French science-fantasy comic.

I guess I've been practicing with my powers again after saving that kid, but the void really threw me. Maybe I'd better leave this stuff to others.

I reserve the right to use slipstream folds outside of academia in the future though.

Bus

[DOCTOR M]

Annabelle, would you come to my office during fourth period today? I need your input on something. The PA mic is covered in pinions (feathers). I can't use it

Thanks, Doctor M (principal)

[DOCTOR M]

Daily step count: 15,033

Personal diary

A mindful hath befallen Paranormal School 13

No, no. That was an autocorrect. I meant "windfall." Wind. Fall.

Because Grace found some money in the expense account earmarked for "Nintendos" [sic] and that's not a real thing we buy at the school. Students must bring their own! But only on acceptable occasions, like free days or the annual March sleepover in the Infinite Labyrinth.

I was in my office, and I knew it not only was a windfall, but a big one, because of the surprised noise Grace made. It was like a screech or a fox barking. It's similar to the noise she makes when she tweezes a particularly painful noise hair.

Grace must never read this.

Anyway, we now have several hundred thou. Whoever put this into the budget must have wanted quite a few Nintendos [sic]! What to buy? New tile for the 300 building? A fresh coat of paint on the baseball field equipment shed. Chain-link fencing??

Ooh, we should buy a new Moonside Bus contract. The current one is acting up, even by Moonside Bus Corp. bus standards.

Paranormal School 13

I must acknowledge that the discrepancy bugs me. Not with the bus, with the budget.

There's a part of me that always yearns for an audit in moments like these, to set things right. We do the budget for the next year every spring and it is quadruple-checked before we send it off to be approved by the Paranormal School Admin. But by the time we're closing on the end of winter there's always something off. Maybe this is the year I let things slide and save myself one weekend of paperwork.

Hoping this discussion today gets the superintendent out of my inbox for five minutes. Seems like it shouldn't be a job for a student, but wasn't I a mere sophomore when I brought those hostages back from Buenos Aires?

[Mikey12]

Lots of people recognize me in the normal world because I was one of the "Campin' Twelve." You might not know about them because you're not from Northern California or something. Well, the Campin' Twelve was a group of co-ed Woodland Explorer Scouts who were in a summer camp that was shut down for corruption, child labor, and deforestation.

Let me break it all down for you, since I'm assuming you haven't seen the news broadcast or watched a YouTube documentary.

We all got sent to a disciplinary camp that was also a summer camp. I didn't do anything wrong. My best friend at the time Bobby Malkewski set me up and made it look like I'd snuck into a cordoned off museum exhibit to vandalize it.

Well, the parents didn't buy it, so I ended up at this discipline camp. But let me tell you it wasn't really a discipline camp, it was actually a horrible work camp where we had to cut down trees. And I'm not talking like with an axe so we could learn. I mean they had forty or fifty kids operating heavy machinery—cutting tractors, chipper belts, and an actual mill.

One thing led to another, and eventually, me and the smallest, most adorable kid at camp, Mew, discovered that we were actually looking for a magic grove inside a haunted forest. We had to run deep into the grove to escape the evil camp counselors and the mysterious Judge

Jordon Bigg (who owned the camp) and then we found the Spirit of the Forest. She was sixteen.

Sorry, I'm getting off track, I'm trying to keep this concise but there was a lot. So eventually, there was a big adventure and me and Mew restored the Heart of the Forest jewel to its keystone and Judge Bigg burst into a cloud of wood sap vapor when he tried to carry the Heart of the Forest outside of the grove. The police came to take away the camp leadership because they were, to a person, escaped convicts. And Mew and my families got a ton of money and that's how my family moved to San Jose.

[Kyle Lemley]

I want pizza.

Does anyone else want pizza?

I know we don't have the best pizza in the country but it's *our* pizza. Los Angeles pizza.

Pizza has a ton of uses. You can eat it. You can sell it for fundraiser funds at two bucks a slice. You can gift pizza to Miss Konrath in hopes of wooing her. She won't go with a student to Winterween but asking is its own reward.

Pizza can even be used to fill out the daily word count requirement in English class. Not pizza itself, rumination on pizza.

[Kyle Lemley]

Actually wait, I have a question.

Why is it that a magic adept can conjure bread, and some types of cheese, and even a tomato, but they can't make a pizza? You can't conjure a pizza for some reason, and I'm gonna go ahead and say thats dumb and doesn't make sense. You can conjure baked goods (bread). You can conjure complex dairy products (cheese). You can conjure plant things (tomato). You can conjure pop tarts.

Why not pizza?

Portals

[Natalie Lavigne]

I've been given a <u>special project</u> by the school!

    More special than SFS, I mean. How exciting.

    I'm supposed to use my portals to investigate the last known location of Paranormal School 12. (!)

    We all heard about it when the school vanished last year, with all students and faculty inside. Well, it sounds like I may be able to help! I have a lot going on, but if it brings back all those people from wherever they went, I'm going to do it!

    Between Japanese classes after school, rugby, mentoring, and advanced English reading, I'm not sure how I'm going to have time for all this. Heck, I've already started getting loose with how I refer to my powers. Are they portals or are they folds? Are they gates or vortexes? Ha, I'll never tell.

    The technical term is slipstream folds.

    But I usually call them portals now. If I am being honest. It just feels right.

Portals

[Natalie Lavigne]

As part of my special search for PS12, they've given me an official file on what happened. I don't see anything about it being confidential, so I guess I'll write a little about it.

PS12 is (was?) located in upstate New York and served supernaturally abled students from the tri-state area. It wasn't located on cursed ground or below any known stellar alignment spirals (a common source of problems for the Paranormal School System). The school wasn't having any issues with ancient evils or rogue former students. There wasn't even an evil student organization, like we have here with the Skullhunters.

They did have a rival school. A Kyoto International Supernatural Institute branch located a few miles away. KISI and PS12 would play rugby and zero-G water polo games in the same league along with a bunch of ordinary schools in the town. Sounds like it was fun coming up with excuses as to why reality got all watery when normal people walked onto the school grounds. KISI students have a private Discord where they talked a lot of trash about PS12, but they also sent search parties and held a vigil. I don't think it's quite the same kind of rivalry as we have here with Santa Monica Underground.

There's exactly one security camera recording in the file, of the front entrance and main hallway, but it's not really clear what's happening. There's this visible energy discharge that doesn't look like anything psychic or magical, and it doesn't look like my portals, so it's unlikely dimensional flimflam is at work. It's just this thin black line with a sort of white outline around it that stretches across the school seal set into the floor and... then it's black.

One thing I noticed: If you switch the camera file over to infrared, the line is a lot fatter, and it moves around like waves in the ocean.

Anyway, today I try opening some folds, starting with the space the school campus was in. I'll keep posting.

[Natalie Lavigne]

Results of the first tests:

Portal 1: Opened at the space facing the front doors of the school at the education fountain shown on the school's intranet website.
 Result: Empty dirt field, like the surface of Mars.

Portal 2: Opened in the space where the football field is, which should give a view back towards their 300 building (which looks way nicer than ours in archival photos).
 Result: Empty field, at a different point.

Portal 3: Opened in Principal McGowan's antechamber, at a point requested by Doctor M. In the Doctor's words, "facing the charter scrolls."
 Results: Empty field. I recognize some of the weeds from Portal 1.

Okay, three cross-country portals are enough to give a girl a seriously dizzy feeling. Enough for today.

Annabelle and some dimensionally enabled seniors were debating what to call our slipstream folds when I walked up to their table in the library. I guess I'm the only one who thinks they should be called portals. But now they agree. That is the magic of being charming and scrappy.

Homework time.

[Alexa Garcia]

Hey, Natalie. Can I ask a question?

I've been reading these, and I'm confused. Why did PS12 disappear? Someone said to me that my nemesis or whatever did it. But I guess they don't actually know?

Oh, speaking of, I went to the library the other day to find out about Lurkett (aforementioned Nemesis), and I couldn't find anything new about her. Can you help? Is she an ancient evil? Maybe from another dimension? Is someone somewhere going to explain the Annual Titan Power Rankings list (of which she is #3)?

Am I going to be asking questions for the rest of my life? But about things there are no answers to? I'm resigned to the fact that I won't get to know the meaning of life, or where my parents are now, or why my little brother is such a jerk to me. Can we get some clarity in here?

I think that's the lyric to a song.

Can- we- get- some- claaaaaa-rity in heeeere?

[Cole Abrams]

Nat,

Did you read the new SFS guidelines they just sent out? They really added to them this year. Rules for engagement up the wazoo, especially for wizards.

You been good?

[Natalie Lavigne]

Sir,

No, I did not. It sounds intense.
British Campire version: bloody in-tents.
Do you get it? Tell me you got that.
Things are peachy, busy tho. Gotta go.

[Cole Abrams]

Yes, I got it. Weird and funny. Well done. Do you want to come by after school and go over this thing? I haven't seen you in like two months, and we have to sign off that we've read it for Madame X to keep us active.

[Natalie Lavigne]

I can't tonight. My parents are back in town, and they want to have dinner with me, probably. Then, portals.

[Cole Abrams]

Fine, understood.

Portals

[Natalie Lavigne]

I had to rush to finish the last five math problems on my homework. After making those portals in the garage, I basically went to my room, crawled into bed, and passed out.

I stopped by the office this morning to drop off notes for Doctor M. Grace said I looked tired. Thanks, Grace. You look great, too.

Maybe there's nothing to find by opening portals to the location PS12 was occupying. I wonder if there's another way to go about it.

Oh, snap. The report on the Mind Wars is due in fourth period. Glad I did that all-nighter Saturday on it.

[Natalie Lavigne]

It's 1:11 a.m. I was just having the best dream. Best as in, unique. Not actually good.

I was in the halls of Paranormal School 12. I recognized lots of faces. Annabelle, Cole, Mrs. Konrath. It was basically everyone from PS13 but at school at PS12.

It was May last year, so I knew the school was about to disappear.

We were in their entry hallway by the offices, like the camera footage. I was standing directly over the big seal on the ground that says "imperare sibi maximum imperium est." This woman with really short black hair dressed in flowing white robes swoops out of the office and slings a fistful of gray powder onto the circle in the middle of the seal and everything starts glowing in lines like in *Tron* (do you remember *Tron*?).

Students shield themselves from indoor magic wind and make their way to class. A crystal sphere rises out of the ground as the rest of the seal recedes, forming a spiral staircase down into the earth. I jump up to ground level as the sphere sparks purple and the blue skies outside turn black, as if someone killed the lights.

Here, in the glow of fluorescent emergency lights, the school shrinks around us. But we stay the same size! The doors are too small to crawl through. When I'm crouched down, pushing lockers away with my elbows, and the pressure starts to hurt, I wake up.

It's past two now. I'm not even tired. I can't believe how real it all felt. Was I just there? Did I see something no one has seen outside of the school?

[Cole Abrams]

Nat, what is going on with you? Why won't you just talk to me? Got some regrets? Maybe? Find a better source of attention?

Nah, never mind. Forget it.

[Natalie Lavigne]

I did another series of portal tests this morning and I tried something new. I made a normal size portal on my side but visualized the exit portal as a matching circle, but just one inch across.

What I saw over at the former location of PS12 was grass as tall as trees! Um, I'm actually not sure if you're supposed to do this with portals, but I figured it would work. And lo, it did.

What if that dream I had was a vision and not just random brain noise? Then maybe what happened is the school shrunk! Is anyone looking for a microscopic PS12 somewhere in that field? Or who knows where it is now? Maybe a hawk took it away and it's in a nest in one of the trees. I've been looking for hours now, but when something is that tiny the odds of finding it in the first few portals is miniscule.

I'd taken a few steps into the grass forest, but I wobbled on my legs and decided I should get ready for school.

I forgot about the group paper on Nellie Pratseva. I didn't even start writing my part. I can barely remember her autobiography. I think she was a witch who found a bunch of stuff out about physics.

It doesn't matter. I can take the B. I can weather the (truly surprised) reaction from my paper partners. I'm back to opening portals today after school. I can feel it, I'm so close.

I should take a shower

[Ms. Cartwright, Teacher]

I'm starting to worry about Natalie. When she was in my class she was dedicated and lighthearted. Jocks, nerds, screamos, mole people—everyone liked her. She was likable but also extraordinarily studious. The ideal from the perspective of a teacher.

But something is going on. I saw her in the hall today and she seemed morose and distracted. Was her turn to teenage angst just delayed? I was pretty sure she was there already, and all the rebellious passion got focused into, uh, social activities.

I am going to have a talk with her.

[Natalie Lavigne]

Sunrise. I'm back to portals. I made another twenty so far to see if I can find a little tiny PS12 somewhere in the tall grass.

Does anyone else find it amusing that KISI and us and lots of other schools have student Discords? I bet Silicon Valley knows so much about the supernatural world simply because they can see all our private groups. Maybe they're all psychics and witches.

[Annabelle Yes]

Natalie, my mentee,

I like this wild look you've taken on. Where did you get your hair done? Very rogue.

Uh, also I waited for you at our spot under the oak tree at lunch, but you didn't come. Do you need a hand with the special project maybe?

[Natalie Lavigne]

Look, can I just say something?

I really appreciate all the concern but if one more teacher or someone comes up to me and is like, "Hey, are you okay?" I'm going to have a cynipton.

Conyption.

Connipion.

Conniption.

I'm just doing something important for a little while. Yes, I can handle it. And no, I probably won't find a tiny little PS12 with all our friends and fellow weirdos, but what if I did?? What if I could save them???

[Annabelle Yes]

Nat,

You've missed three meetings we had planned. And you won't answer your phone, and your homeroom teacher says you weren't here yesterday either.

Where are you?

Portals

[Louis Air]

SFS Student Incident Report
No. 1719-2023-N

Summary: I went to go check on Nat and things got wild in a bad way.

Request Extra Credit? Check this box: [give give]

Detailed Description:

Natalie Lavigne (Class of '24) didn't show for two separate mentor lunches with Annabelle Yes. Anna reached out to me at SFS. I checked around, her teachers also said she'd been gone for two days.

I went to her home (1008 Effie) to find that her parents were not home, and the front door was unlocked.

Per SFS protocol I notified my partner, Cole, to indicate I was going into an unresponsive environment so he could monitor me via my bracelet.

It was weird Cole didn't want to come with me. But whatever, you do you. I know he's got drama with Nat.

He won't read this, right?

I pushed open the door and found the living area was fancy and furnished with rich people furniture and pots and stuff (a harp?). Butterflies of a variety of sizes fluttered in the air in front of me. Like, normal butters and butters as big as a book and butters the size of a little fly.

I went up the stairs to what I figured was Nat's room (colorful but orderly) and the butterfly density went way way up. Upon opening the door to her room, I was knocked over by a small dragon. I activated standard defensive barriers for large creatures (slippery psychic barriers, a chant that makes you taste bad) and called Cole for help.

But as I crawled back towards the stairs, I looked back and that wasn't a dragon! That was a normal garden lizard. But really, really big. It crawled away on the ceiling towards another room, and I went back to Nat's room.

Inside, I saw a slipstream fold reaching from floor to ceiling (ten-foot diameter), edges fraying as evidence it hadn't been maintained in some time. The opening led to a craggy landscape where blades of grass were mountains. From what I could see, a footpath led down into rocky ground and to what appeared to be a tiny staircase.

The portal remains open, stabilized by a rotating team of SFS students using restricted item 11700-V on loan with special permission from the Restricted Zone Safety Cabinet. Natalie has been reported missing to the school.

We should do an expedition through the portal to search for Nat and her parents. Cole has also volunteered finally.

Portals

[Cole Abrams]

SFS Student Incident Report
   No. 1719-2022-N

Summary: Louis and I plus a faculty member went through the black hole in Natalie's room and brought her back.

Request Extra Credit? Check this box: [X]

Detailed Description:

Louis and I reported to the faculty SFS Supervisor by way of the vertically oriented big screen TV in the SFS lounge. Appearing only by spooky backlit silhouette, Madame X listened to Louis describe the portal at Nat's house and okayed our expedition into the slipstream fold to go search for her. In an unexpected twist, Madame X also said she would be coming and left the screen. A door to the next classroom over opened and Madame X walked out. She is apparently a silhouette in real life. It's not just a spooky lighting thing from when we talk to her.

I also attempted to scan her, and she has a level of psychic barrier I've never felt before. It was like I wasn't even a foot away from her when I was kicked back. I'm sorry, Doctor M, I know you want to know more about her.

We used a slipstream fold created by Madame X to go directly to the Lavigne household back yard/pool area, where we could hear Nat's window rattling on the second floor from unstable fold energy. We jimmied the back door and went upstairs, where we reported to Mabel, who was doing homework while she maintained the slipstream fold.

Madame X did not speak this entire time. She simply looked at Louis, and then me, and Louis rattled off details about the portal.

We cast basic defensive barriers on ourselves (an impact barrier and a chant that makes you taste bad) and went into the portal.

The exit portal, as Louis had calculated, measured four millimeters in diameter, making us two to three millimeters tall. Weeds and stuff were super big and there was a canyon of sorts leading down into the ground. In the distance, it appeared to stop at a man-made step of some kind. Louis said it was a staircase, but it was far enough away that it could have been a trick of the light.

We made our way down the canyon and noted that when we were super tiny sounds were strange. For example, a bird sounded more like a dragon might in an expensive fantasy TV show. The distant drone of cars on suburban streets were like long droning storm fronts.

Madame X does not appear to make footsteps, by the way. She floated behind Louis and me.

We reached the end of the canyon and Louis was right, it did appear to be a worn staircase leading down into the earth, framed on either side by thick bunches of grass trees. The staircase looked like marble or something and the steps had beat up, disintegrating grip strips in them, like what might have been at PS12. We asked Madame X for comment, and she said nothing.

Louis and I took this time, based on how creepy and ominous this school stairwell stretching down into darkness was, to don extra protection (subdermal and elemental barriers, incantation to increase odds of tasting bad to wider range of things).

At this size a school campus that measured a block to a side would be about seventy centimeters by seventy centimeters—very small but more than big enough to be seen at normal size. So of course, the only way this could have remained hidden is if it were underground.

We had been descending for some time (five, maybe ten minutes) when we began to see brighter light up ahead and could hear something. Eventually, we reached a landing where we found Nat unconscious. It was just floor and dirt walls and ceiling, with no further passages to anywhere. We used basic safety to check her vitals and I carried her back up. Madame X said nothing the entire time and did nothing until we were back at the Lavigne household, and she opened a portal to the hospital for us to take Nat.

Louis pointed out that Natalie had been laying across a crest on the floor, with Latin on it. Later we looked it up. It was the crest in the entryway of Paranormal School 12—imperare sibi maximum imperium est. "To rule yourself is the ultimate power."

Portals

The portal in Nat's room collapsed from entropic decay about ten minutes after we stepped back through it. We marked the location where it opened at the former location of PS12 for further investigation.

I wish I hadn't ignored her. I was mad, I screwed up. Ugh.

[Natalie Lavigne]

Back to school today.

Being in class feels weird, all those other eyes and words and quiet. I spent so much time exploring through crackling energy circles to strange places, that the idea that I'm supposed to sit still and write on paper or read is really strange. It's even stranger sitting at lunch with Annabelle under the tree. I think I did a bunch of portal things she's never done. It's like she's not the expert anymore.

The missed classwork has reared its head too. The grades will take a hit, which means a lengthy conversation with the parents. When they are back.

I think what I'm supposed to do here is be upbeat and lighthearted but this is serious, right? I failed. And I don't like it. At all.

Well, I'm better at making portals. Or, I mean, I'm still the same as I was before my little expedition, but that's a big improvement over where I was even just a couple of weeks ago. But now I'm afraid. I mean, I can make those things go anywhere! I don't trust myself. I could open a portal and just leave. Bye, parents. Bye, school. Cut all the little threads that connect me to here and...

Last night, when I was sitting in my room at my vanity, I may have opened up a teeny, tiny, little, thimble-sized portal. Just to make sure my homework from yesterday was still there on top of Ms. Cartwright's homework stack.

It was.

So maybe just little portals for now.

Oh. Cole. I should call him.

[Mikey12]

One weird thing is I can't see my scars ever because of all this gray fur on my bod. I'm so used to seeing them in the mirror after a shower, dashed lines from my shoulder down at an angle.

They're still there though. I just brushed the fur out of the way, and I can see the one in front of my shoulder. It's a lot bigger now.

NM, this wasn't worth a post! Promise better content next time.

[Phoebe Case]

Well now it's happened. The stupid web zone masters won't let me get my website up because a beekeeper (?) stole it and put up a bee ranch website.

What does bee farming have to do with cracked cases? I can't get anyone on the phone at the web masters.

[Mikey12]

Hey, Pheebs, if you let the website hosting lapse, someone probably just scooped it up. It happens. I used to have spindoctors.net (to expose the *truth* and the people *spinning* it) but then someone got it when I was grounded from the computer and now a guy is squatting on it trying to sell it to a music person?

I don't understand music. It's too obvious how it does mind control stuff. It's not just me, about three quarters of the population can't hear beats. They just pretend to, so they won't be embarrassed.

[Phoebe Case]

So, you're saying I can get the website back from the bees?

[Mikey12]

I mean, yeah. Just go ask.
   Unless of course, you want to uncover the *truth*.

[Phoebe Case]

I don't understand. Are you suggesting that there is a conspiracy at the bee ranch?
   Does anyone know how I can get out of my Tesla? I played Facebook for too long and it died.

[Cole Abrams]

Still in a funk about Natalie but she reached out and it seems like we are at least not enemies. I still don't trust her.
   And so, I spend my days at home with Mom and Harry and the sisters.
   I think my family is pretty good, but sometimes I do have little selfish wishes. Like I wish sometimes that there weren't eight of us. I'm sure Mom didn't plan on having quintuplets when she was forty-one. And I wouldn't trade those little demons for anything. Mina, Margo, Malia, Mel, and Bridget are really the best. And each is special in their own way. And they really do change fast.
   I guess I think it'd be nice to have a real girlfriend or whatever. I mean, I go on a lot of dates and stuff, but they're always in a group.

What if there was someone who was just one hundred percent mine and I was one hundred percent theirs? And then we still had our lives and stuff, but we were like exoplanetary bodies that orbit each other while they also orbit their star.

I can't remember what that's called, but I am sure that's a thing.

[Cole Abrams]

Found it. Those are binary planets, and they are theoretical, not unlike the idea of me having a girlfriend.

Haha, that came out a bit cynical. I'm okay, everyone.

Oh, wristband is buzzing. Be back.

[Adult Lyle]

Cole, my friend! You'll never believe who I ran into.

Short version of a long story: Shadow Joe stumbled into my cafe the other day with a messed-up hand. I think it was from working on his 1969 Toyota 2000GT, but as you know Shadow Joe cannot (or won't) talk. Best guess is he was installing some sort of illegal nitro boost system. He does this sort of thing, but I don't know what for. Shadow Joe has a lot going on under that jet-black trench coat and wide-brimmed hat.

So off to the hospital we went, and who was there to help with paperwork but your mom! I always say to know a person is to meet their parents, and then also meet that person. Haha, I'm just messing with you.

Or am I? Truth is, she's really great. She took super good care of Joe and when she found out I knew you she said some really nice things. Not just mom praise. She thinks you're a good guy and you're destined for greatness.

I know you're looking for that special someone, and don't worry. I'm not saying your special someone is your mom! That would be messed up. But if the goal is to build a home with someone, well, that's pretty rad. And in the meantime, maybe consider that you have a perfectly good home to start with. It just might be a little chaotic sometimes.

Oh, Shadow Joe walked in and his other hand is messed up. Gotta goes. Like I said, sometimes home can be chaotic.

Field Trip^3

[Camel Riboy]

Who else is SUPER PUMPED about the big field trip to Las Vegas? I'm going to climb on top of that one big thingy in the center of the farm, just like in my mom's yearbook picture!

That's a weird thing happening to your face in that old picture, mom! Smiling? You??? NoooOOOoo.

[Nouto Hashimoto]

Oh yeah, I remember that trip. It was so sick. I climbed on top of the biggest cube and jumped off and tucked and rolled on the rubberized playground material. Kids have too much fun, but if you play your cards right, you might get to have a little fun also as an old.

[Alexa Garcia]

Wait.
    We go to Las Vegas? The sophomores all get to go to Las Vegas?
    Is that even allowed? Do the parents know about this?

Field Trip^3

[Kelli Konrath, CEED]

A quick reminder to you sophomores who like to leave it to the last minute: If you don't bring your signed permission slip, you are absolutely not going to the Farm. And you're going to miss a whole bushel of (math) fun.

I'm going because my legal guardian (me, I am an adult) signed my permission slip.

[DOCTOR L]

It seems there is some confusion about the annual sophomore trip to the Sunbeam Cube Farm outside of Las Vegas.

We would not let students roam the Las Vegas Strip or (worse!) the Fremont Street Experience unsupervised. I'm not a moron.

You know who is a moron though? The students who don't go on this trip! So, get your permission slips signed and make sure you go by Nurse Millard's to get your inoculations.

Prepare for fun. Prepare for the Cube Farm.

[Alexa Garcia]

Okay, so abuelita said no to the trip. Her actual words—translated to english—were "as long as I am alive, you are not going to Las Vegas."

The weird thing is I said what the permission slip said to say and pointed out it was in the

"Las Vegas area" and will NOT be in the city. But no.

I don't even want to go, so this is fine I think.

[Alexa Garcia]

Okay, so confession time. I forged my grandma's signature. I don't know. It's a field trip and my whole grade is going, so shouldn't I go, too? I'm done with this whole dancing around other people and their stupid feelings. Even her.

We leave tomorrow, so I'll just discretely pack a backpack and bake myself some cookies that look like grandma made them. Better to ask forgiveness? I read that online.

[Alexa Garcia]

We're back! A lot fewer classmates went than I thought would go, but hey! Still a pretty good number, including a ton of people I didn't recognize.

Rogue softmores!

[Mabel Avagyan]

That was so fun! This was absolutely worth the trouble of getting my father to sign the permission slip.

[Alexa Garcia]

The bus is outside as I type this. I wonder what cube farms are actually like. Here goes nothing.

I've been hauling my backpack with my field trip things with me all day so it will be nice to stow it in a bus.

[Alexa Garcia]

Wait a minute. I'm back but I just posted the thing I remember writing when I left. Am I…

[Alexa Garcia]

Holy smokes. I just crept up to the window next to the library and looked, and I'm actually in there putting stuff in my backpack! I think those of us who went on the field trip arrived back before we left.

I just traveled through time. I'm a time traveler.

I think, anyway. It's hard to tell here. Should I tell a teacher? Yes?

Field Trip^3

[Mabel Avagyan]

Why is there an annoying, younger version of me posting to my Snap?

Do not interact with her.

[Damien Cross]

Man, is traffic always this bad on the way to Vegas? I thought you could drive there from LA in like an hour, but we are *crawling* up this mountain.

I wonder if there's some crypts and stuff up here.

Will there be time at the Cube Farm to E.X.P.L.O.R.E.?

[Mabel Avagyan]

I don't think this is Las Vegas. I think it's close but when I go to look it up on my phone, I can't get a signal. Maybe there's WiFi in the big barn where they have lunch and dinner here. I guess a guy is gonna play spoons in concert with the dissonant warbling of the smallest hypercube at the farm. "Li'l Right Angles," it says on the brochure.

Sounds sick.

[Alexa Garcia]

Well.

I'm home thirty minutes after we left for the Cube Farm. Which means I guess I'm still on that bus. So, I guess I can tell you what is going to happen on the trip.

Turns out only forty or fifty students ended up getting permission (or bluffing), so the crowd was small. We threw a tennis ball around with our minds and yell-sang songs and made trucks do big honks when they drove by the bus. Monika came (her foster family are alumni, I did not know) and this little weird guy with a mustache and widow's peak named Gomez and a bunch of people I didn't know, but now I do.

After a bunch of mountains and cars and desert, we ended up over the state line and exited at some place called Henderson, and we drove out east for a long time until way after it was dark. We finally pulled up at this little ranch with desert plants and a little cluster of wooden buildings. It kinda made me think of this field trip we went on when I was little to a fake old-timey town place that had a blacksmith and a pumpkin patch and stuff. Except here all the old-timey townspeople wore these uniforms with blinking green lights on their belts and there were these transparent cages with weird jittery cubes in them.

They led us to a barn that had been converted into a bunkhouse hotel thing and everyone got a little bunk room to share. Monika and I were roommates, and she called the top bunk. I didn't say anything, but I felt weird sharing the bunk. Whatever.

Then we went back out and we started a tour of the farm. The clear cages held all kinds of different strange cubes. One had a swirling indigo cube energy vortex in it, and another had a 4-D Hypercube, folding infinitely in on itself. We learned about some of the more dangerous and crazy cubes that're out there, from other dimensions or whatever.

[Alexa Garcia]

We're supposed to be asleep in the bunks and I can't sleep. So, of course I've been thinking a lot about Lurkett.

I mean, seriously, this is so dumb. What am I supposed to do to an angry vengeful demigod? And no one is helping! I'll just add it to the list of stupid nonsense.

I asked Monika about it, and she said in Europe there's tons of stuff like this on the books. Just list after list of bizarre crises/prophecy/showdown criteria. So, it isn't just a California thing.

Anyway, so the second day was learning about this stuff, and then we saw the 4-D Hypercube again (it tried to enchant us, but it was in a... cube... of its own!) and went back.

Field Trip^3

[GOMEZ]

I didn't go to the Cube Farm. I am a junior and it is frowned on to double-dip such an experience. But I must have somehow been on this trip because I actually remember talking to Alexa and the tennis ball floating.

    I went last year when I was a sophomore. So, I guess she was there last year?

[DOCTOR M]

Daily step count: 15,030

    It seems there is some confusion about an annual sophomore trip to the Sunbeam Cube Farm outside of Las Vegas.

    We would not let students visit such a dangerous place. Hypercubes, even ones confined into our meagre reality, have a knack for mucking up the flow of ordinary time and getting theirs.

    My predecessor chartered such an overnight field trip once in the 2000s. But it was such a disaster they never did another one. There's a file in the restricted wing of the library about the trip and ensuing damage control (dimensional, parental). It was one of the first rogue transgressions of a certain Moonside Bus I'd very much like to get rid of, but who will not allow the paperwork to be completed.

    One thing that always confused me: There were only six students in 2004 who managed to get a permission slip signed (or who were foolish enough to forge a signature). But they all reported a bus full of dozens of students.

    Over the years, the slow trickle of participants adds up though. Adds up to a busful?

    Maybe maybe maybe.

    If you do choose to visit the Sunbeam Cube Farm (with an adult guardian's permission), prepare for a cautiously educational overnight experience. Prepare to learn. Carefully. Please.

[Camel Riboy]

So funny story! My mom was actually ON THE BUS, and I WAS THE ONE WHO TOOK THE PICTURE OF HER from her yearbook?!

We are somehow on that 2004 field trip at the same time and we are both SOPHOMORES.

We wear the SAME SIZE PANTS. There was a CLOTHING EXCHANGE.

It brought us CLOSER TOGETHER. Honestly I thought she was a boring jerk but when she was my age we were a couple of sister bros.

THANK YOU, CUBES!

Although now that I think about it, she didn't tell me I was going on her trip, and it was a time loop. She's been lying to me for almost TWENTY YEARS?!

[Alexa Garcia]

Okay, so I guess the trip *didn't* happen.

Also, it *did*.

And I went on the trip in 2004. When I wasn't born.

With a lot of other PS13 students from then and other years.

Does this keep happening forever? A half dozen students are added every year. Does the bus just get infinitely longer? It did seem like a long bus, but definitely not out of the ordinary.

I guess theoretically there wouldn't be a PS13 to send students from at some point in the future, due to the heat death of the universe or the opening of a new campus.

I'm not going to worry about it anymore.

[Janelle Avagyan]

So, after a lengthy conversation with our parents, Doctor M, Mrs. Konrath, and a college admissions advisor, I've opted to stay in this time and treat the other Mabel as a big sister. I'm going by Janelle because I always liked the name. Dad is turning his home office into a bedroom for me. I've never had a sister before! It used to be just me and the parents. I'm really excited.

Sometimes this wacky world gives you lemons and your ghost parts just decide, "NO, TWICE AS MANY LEMONS!"

And then you just gotta deal with it.

[Alexa Garcia]

I can't say I'm jealous of all these weird connections to come out of the trip. Sisters fight worse than brothers. Them girls can't be trusted.

[Camel Riboy]

I don't think my parents will let me go. Isn't it dangerous there with all the mobsters?

[Kelli Konrath, CEED]

Every once in a while I'll be grading a big ol' stack of algebra tests and there will be a lone Cube Farm permission slip stuck in there from a year between 2004 and now. It is almost always obviously forged.

When I was a student (PS6! Maple Leafs Represent!) I always thought I could forge a pretty good parent signature in a pinch. Study the genuine article, dust it psychically with a vague feeling of authenticity, create a distraction for the coach when you hand it in…

Either kids have gotten worse at it or I was completely wrong.

In other news, I have my first 2023 slip now. Forged again.

Gotta catch 'em all. The cubes demand it. (No, they don't.)

[Zone Smith]

Oh, nards I'm so borked.

    Has anyone seen Newt? I just had her in history and then she was gone.

    Oh man, oh man, why did I ask to borrow her?

[Upton Lopez]

Hey, don't freak out.

[Bert the Third]

Did you check in the choir room? Newt loves pianos.

[Zone Smith]

Newt is not there, man! Newt, if you're reading this, please come back. I'm gonna get in so much trouble.

[JR Benton]

Anyone see that mouse reading that little book in the library? What the hoosiers was that?

[MADAME X]

My pet hamster is missing.

[MADAME X]

I will clarify. The hamster is unusually smart and charismatic by hamster standards. The issue is hamsters are illegal in California and I risk causing an ecological apocalypse if she is not returned.

...
1000101x n0n10010 11101y1y x11n0101 x1011110 nxx10y01

Best Friend Tryouts

[Gertrude Baumgartner]

Tryouts for being my new best friend start tomorrow. If you think you've got what it takes to be one of us, I want to know!

Edit: I'm getting some flack, so I want to say something. You all don't know how tough it is being a wooden doll. Joints need constant maintenance. I can't do backflips reliably. So maybe before you go out of your way to say that I suck, think about your opinions, and how mean they are. #bestfriends

[MAX Rushmore]

Does Gertrude accept best friend applications from guys too? I am assuming she wants another friend that is some girl. I would throw my palm against the big red button, but I don't want to get shot down by the most popular girl in school.

Also assuming maybe she would prefer a wooden doll friend, but I know only a couple come here and the rest go to SMURSH because that's where you go if you're a wooden doll from a wealthy family.

I am always up for new experiences! Challenge me!

Best Friend Tryouts

[Esmerelda]

Yo, best friends doll girl! We can help each other. See me at lunch.

-E

PS, I am aware of the little gang sneaking into my locker to get at my homework tutor. You have been warned. She's mine. I use her for help with spells. Not you.

[Gertrude Baumgartner]

Today is the big day for one lucky person. It is time to lay down some ground rules.

    1. I only have space for one new best friend, but a runner-up might become a new acquaintance.

    2. You do not have to be a wooden doll, but yes, DJ, I would like for it to be a girl, because we all know boys and girls can't just be friends. Even if they were both dolls!

    3. The primary metric by which I judge my best friend is whether they can keep a secret. As such, there will be a little obstacle course set up in the theater for you to navigate. It will be arduous. Yes, very, very hard. You will want to ask for help, and Maria will be there standing beside you, ready to free you from the terrible predicament you may or may not wind up in. But to help you, she will ask you for a secret I have given you at random from my actual list of dark secrets at the start of this course.

    4. If you reveal the secret, you will be freed, but forfeit the course and my possible best-friendship.

Okay, see you all after seventh period. #bestfriends

[Alexa Garcia]

No, I did not compete in the best friend tryouts. I saw part of them though. I had an hour before my internship time.

Who wants a friend that badly? It looked really dangerous, and Gertrude spent a lot of time yelling at people, like it was a reality show. I guess it was set up so that Gertrude told everyone a true secret at the start of the obstacle course. And then when they would be trapped by obstacles (a projected net dangling over a spike pit? Will I be able to do that eventually?), the girl had to give up the secret or face certain doom. And a lot of them did and Gertrude got so mad.

I don't think it occurred to her that telling real secrets would cause many, many, many secrets to get loose into the school. For example, I learned while I was there that: Gertrude does not weather seal herself as much as she should; Gertrude still has a stuffed octopus gift from her newly ex-best friend (one of the other wooden dolls); and Gertrude sneaks out of her house at night to go to parties with SMURSH students, which I am pretty sure is bad. But I also don't go to parties, so what do I know?

In conclusion, who needs a best friend that badly? After much drama and disappointment here, I am totally content with having my friends I see sometimes from my old school, and just being friendly with people here. Like that li'l guy Gomez always bows when he sees me. That's all the friend I need. And I don't need to deal with any extra nonsense.

I saw a flyer for Vulcan's new internship drive. You'd have the same job helping out with Anderton's big secret project. You should totally do it! It's been real fun.

Best Friend Tryouts

[Alexa Garcia]

It's been nice to have all this extra time to research the big fight with one Cupid Lurkett, Esquire, now that I'm not distracted with all that other drama.

I got permission to look at some things in the Restricted Zone and boy is that place dusty. Dusty and a little bit creepy. It's got those low ceilings and the halls are real narrow and in the corner they have a couple of microfish machines, I guess for old newspapers? And then a device that looks like abuelita's sewing magnifier, with the big glass part with a switch-on light on an arm. Except it sits over a perfectly still chrome cylinder? So, you're looking up close at... perfectly smooth metal? Reflecting your huge eyeball?

Maybe it wasn't plugged in. The microfishes weren't.

So, I guess there was a big archive of the Lurkett stuff, a full volume in a whole row of Titan-related things.

And there's a picture of her! It's got those weird colors old film pictures have and she's floating in the air in front of a blue sky that's really mostly filled with smoke. From fires? From her?

In the end what stopped her (me?!) was this mysterious psychic wearing all black who showed up outta nowhere and they jumped up to her in the Valley and did a big karate fight with energy blasts that shut her down. And there was a lot of evidence that it was a psychic that was using some kind of device, so the <u>obvious</u> conclusion was made that they were from the future.

So, here we are. And apparently I'm that psychic, and also Lurkett is maybe coming back now? But also, I have to go back in time to stop her with fighting, even though I still don't know how to fight with my powers. And I guess I should figure out how to get a bus to the Valley in 1994. Do they have old bus maps anywhere?

[ANDERTON NEO]

raises arms triumphantly

It's time, Paranormal School! Tune in tonight!
    I love you all, so much.

                          -Anderton Neo-
                          -XXXXXXXX-
                          -XXXX XXXX-

The Machine

[Synthea Fluffson]

Did you SEE the video from the Vulcan announcement?? They had an audience member come up on stage and used a device to PROJECT THEIR THOUGHTS ONTO A WALL. No psychics needed. No spells needed.

He wasn't kidding when he said he'd used what he learned here to create cool things. We're the key to the future of technology!

[Natalie Lavigne]

I think if I saw that video right, what happened was Anderton got up on stage, stood on a specific spot on this platform, and put his hands on those two glass spheres. And then a machine behind him projected through him. And that somehow got his thoughts onto the wall in visual form.

That sounds right. I mean, it had to have been his real thoughts because they had that curtain set up to fall just in case he thought about something scandalous.

blush

All the normies were freaking out, and that was before Anderton revealed that they were releasing a phone app, Mind Meld, that does the same thing. And ties into their online gadget store, Vulcan, which you might already be using if you think you are mature but actually just *need* gadgets to fill the void.

[Cole Abrams]

Everyone online is exclusively talking about the Mind Meld app announcement video. Everywhere I go it's Mind Meld. The idea of a free app that tells you what you're really thinking, deep down, and what stuff you might really need to buy. It's got people going.

[Damien Cross]

Today when we were going down into Anderton Neo's press conference lair, we balancing on rafters, and I had to dodge a falling cable and ended up hanging over the edge of the rail by one hand.

When I flipped back up who was standing there but famous person Anderton Neo in the flesh.

I've met a lot of famous people but they're all old adventure buddies of my uncle's. I never met a person who made the phone I use or whatever. So I was super nervous. But then he said that my dodge skills were super good. I was so star struck I couldn't even tell him that it was a cursed luck power that runs in the Cross family, and it makes getting a girlfriend really hard.

Anyway, I met Anderton Neo. He's so cool! I'm going to pay more attention in programming class.

[DOCTOR M]

Grace won't shut her trap about Mind Meld. I know, Grace! I need a new grill, too, and I don't need an app to tell me that. I can feel the grill-shaped emptiness in my soul.

Daily step count: 15,039

[Annabelle Yes]

Some of you slept through Introduction to Psychotectonics years ago and you still haven't figured out what you saw in the Mind Meld announcement.

Here's what's going on in that demo. The Mind Meld machine, whatever that thing is, has a special rock in it somewhere that's tuned to just the right frequency, and it can feel the little vibrations caused by someone thinking a certain way. The reason why? That type of thought taps into the part of your brain that talks wirelessly to everyone else's brains through the Matrix (the Internet). Even normies have a two-way link into the Matrix, just not as strong as the psychic one. It's not a place you can go. It's more a place you can holler into and hear from. Figuratively speaking.

Again, I wouldn't be typing this, but Esmerelda honestly didn't remember this stuff even though they've been saying it in PT class for years. Did you think I was part psychic and that's why we're able to talk to each other? No. Obviously, you're tapping into a hidden other world where all the psychic energy flows and we are all connected.

It's pretty simple really. It feels weird somebody didn't think of this already.

I don't really know how the software gets to that realm and turns it into gadget recommendations. I'm sure Anderton Neo has been working on An Algorithm or whatever.

The Machine

[Alexa Garcia]

Okay, so now that everyone knows what I've been helping with, I can talk a little bit more about the Mind Meld machine. The truth is, I'm now one of the key parts of the team.

Yes, really!

So, the machine's ability is a lot like mine, right? I can project thoughts into the world around me. Sometimes even if I don't want to. They actually needed my help, because as a projector, I'm a very rare kind of psychic. They needed me to use the machine for a while first to help test it. Like, they had me hooked up to the glass spheres just like the demos you've seen. And it's not gonna brag, but my mind images were super clear and vivid. Not like their demo online. Crystal clear with a life and vibrancy you wouldn't believe.

People can see what it's like to have my power. Just remember, it's much nicer when you can turn it off. ;)

[ANDERTON NEO]

People the world over are going nuts for Mind Meld (powered by Vulcan). Thank you so much, PS13.

Since the launch is a galactic smash, and so many, many of you have asked, I want to talk a little bit about why I ended up founding Vulcan.

And it's a PS13 story!

Everyone that writes about me on normie websites talks about how I'm warm and generous and clever. Well, it wasn't like that when I was here at PS13. The truth was it was really unpleasant for me here at first. All my tests said I was a normal spectrum psychic. Maybe not as skilled as the spooky kids who end up in Naval Intelligence, but I could do basic things and make a sphere that no noise or light can come out of. Stuff like that.

And I was shy. You can imagine how that was during reading exercises!

The minute I could feel someone's tickly thought tendrils brush up against my mind, I would freak out. It made me so uncomfortable, like they were prying me open to stare at my guts. The other students didn't have a problem with it. It's sort of the core thing about being psychic, isn't it? Let someone in to rummage around in the analog chaos of the human mind (with permission). Rummage through their mind in return (with permission). Bring your opinions about it. Drink wine on the massive pile of detritus you brought with your flawed brain and laugh and leave it when you jump back home.

Detritus is another word for trash. No. Thanks.

I've got enough junk up here on my own. Why would I mix all that up with your junk?

In the reading exercises, the more I fought back, the meaner people were. They didn't want me to hide, and they would be like, "Andy, don't be so scared. Let's find out what's making you fight back," like everything was okay.

Then they'd reach in and would you believe it? It came to light my bike got stolen when I was eight and then they'd want to go deeper and find out why I was so desperately upset and why my bike was sitting out unlocked and what I did about the bike being gone and how I felt about the catastrophic aftermath. What I said it meant about me as a tiny person.

Who cares? It's just a bike. I didn't care then, and I don't now.

The best scanner in the class was Leslie Brooks. She had short black hair and always wore these red jackets, and we got paired together for the final in Brain Connectrics.

She sits down and she says, "It's fine you can trust me." And I honestly was about to have a panic attack because I had a big monster crush on her. In 1999, short black hair and a red leather jacket was about as cool as it got. She looked like someone out of a Blur music video.

And she was about to find out my darkest truth!

They made us come up to the front of the room, and everyone is watching, and the girl I had a crush on was about to reach into my mind and I'm DESPERATE not to let the truth out. But she smiles like it's fine and I'm frozen in my chair and her eyes close, and I can feel

The Machine

those little threads drifting in, and my mind is racing, looking for any excuse at all to get up.

I didn't look like I do now. I was a weird kid, even by PS13 standards. No offense. I weighed about ninety pounds. I had scraggly hair and hadn't started trimming my eyebrows, so they were elaborate and connected. I had a denim shirt and jeans on because no one bothered at home to tell me that you shouldn't ever wear those together.

And then the whole class is waiting for the exercise and Leslie gives me this wry look, and I know I'm doomed. She would tell the class or her friends or whatever. She would save it or say it right away. Or she wouldn't say anything to anyone at all out of pity. But <u>she would know</u> I liked her.

But.

In that moment of crisis, I realized something that I'd never thought of before. While she's in here (I'm pointing at my head!), I can think of new things, <u>and she would see those instead</u>.

The teacher says to begin, and Leslie closes her eyes, and I pictured Leslie and me together. We walked hand in hand up to the top of one of those hilly streets out in the neighborhood, and looked down over Echo Park, and then we let go of each other and walked down opposite sides of the hill alone.

I opened my eyes and...

Leslie's face was as perplexed as they get!

She cocked her head to the side. She didn't say anything about it to the teacher (she told the stolen bike story, like everyone did).

Then after class, she came up to me and the funniest thing happened. She said, "I saw the thing with the hill on Reservoir."

And I said, "So?"

And she knelt next to my desk and whispered, "That was so sad. Who is she?"

Incredible.

Don't you see? She didn't recognize herself.

Maybe it was because we don't see ourselves the way other people do. She didn't know she was cool. And because she didn't, she never even realized I was thinking of her. Or it could have been anything. It doesn't matter. What matters is the redirection had gone perfectly.

So, I said to Leslie, "She's long gone. That's life, I guess," and I left the classroom.

And you know what I did then? I went out that afternoon, broke into my parents' abandoned office complex, and purchased my first web domain. It was the site that would eventually become Scope Creep, which eventually became the juggernaut Vulcan we know and love.

I also got my first pair of black aviators. Dress for the world you want, I always say.

-Anderton Neo-
-Receive the Universe's Wisdom-
-Mind Meld-

[GOMEZ]

So, what happened with the girl, Anderton?

[ANDERTON NEO]

I haven't talked to her since that day. And please, call me Neo!

-Anderton Neo-
-Receive the Universe's Wisdom-
-Mind Meld-

The Machine

[Cole Abrams]

I downloaded Mind Meld and I gotta say, it's really good. I was thinking about... well... Natalie, and then it said what I needed was a graphic novel. I don't really like reading comics that much, but this thing showed up and I really really like it. It's the story of the last woman in a world where all women died surprisingly, and she has to travel across the US with a team of men protecting her.

[ANDERTON NEO]

Hello Paranormal School!

The app really does work by reading the thoughts of any user on the planet. No trickery at work there! It's not so hard to recommend things to tech-savvy people in my generation. Is it new? Is it matte black? Is it a micro-home in Marfa, Texas?

It's yours. Done.

-Anderton Neo-
-Receive the Universe's Wisdom-
-Mind Meld-

[Natalie Lavigne]

Does anyone else get a weird vibe from Anderton? I know his app is the number one store in the world but every time he visits campus to talk to us I look at him and something just feels off, like he's incapable of being angry. Would you trust someone who was incapable of anger?

Uh, anyway. After the conclusion of the PS12 investigation, I've been mostly keeping to myself. I saw some SFS friends today and said hi, but they were called away to deal with some kind of crisis around a book report test in Ms. Cartwright's class.

It feels weird not being in the mix.

[Alexa Garcia]

I used the machine today and something different happened.

I was having a bad day and I went into Vulcan and Anderton was there at his ergonomic standing desk, and he saw me. I must have looked miserable, so he asked what was wrong and I wouldn't say. He nodded and said to come with him. He led me down to the hallway behind the organic snacks counter with the keycode locks. Behind that was this empty room with plain concrete floors that had one of the Mind Meld machines.

He insisted I try it, and I said that I had already (I helped him test it!). He got all goofy and said he was sorry, that he had forgotten. He said he wanted me to do something a little bit different, and instead of thinking of <u>something</u>, he wanted me to focus on whatever it was inside that felt bad. Whatever that feeling of "loneliness or anger or whatever it might be" was. To focus on it and imagine it coming out of my mind.

So, I went to the clear glass round parts and put my hands on them, and the machine made a noise and the platform under my feet vibrated. The projector screen flickered like it does, but instead of a picture of a cupcake or of clouds or a naked person (which happens so, so much by the way), the image looked just like the room we were in.

Except.

Except except except...

Then <u>I</u> appeared on the other side. In the image. And the copy of me took her hands off the silver thing and she looked so sad! Just like I had felt. No, way way worse. She looked miserable.

And I felt fine.

God, that reflection looked wretched. I don't think I've felt like she looked, since that night when I fought with Bianca. Other Alexa just sat there with tears streaming down her face, trying to cheer up, trying to force the tears back in, and failing at it. She just kept going with the tears and the little hiccup sobs. It was weird to see, especially because I didn't feel remotely miserable anymore.

Sad-me projected a gray environment around my reflection that

The Machine

began to rain. Thunder rumbled and lightning flashed somewhere hidden from view. It was more detailed and vaster than any projection I've ever done.

And I laughed. Because it really was ridiculous.

Anderton switched the machine off and said, "Sometimes all it takes is a little 'mindfulness' when we're feeling down."

And the screen with sad-me on it faded. He used his admin code to give me Swedish Fish from the snack counter and I went to do intern things. And honestly ever since I've felt great.

This is the best thing that's happened in a long time.

[Adult Lyle]

Natalie, you left your binder here at Bandido's. Um, Bandido Cafe. I think it's a planner. It's full of scheduling stuff. Looks important! Please come by and grab it.

[Natalie Lavigne]

My planner! I will be by in a half hour, after knife throwing class.

[Adult Lyle]

Hey, Natalie! Good catching up with a busy bee like yourself.

I've been thinking about what you said. And you know what? I gotta disagree. I don't think planning things out a lot makes a big difference all of the time. It does help. If I didn't order coffee beans when I needed them, I'd never be able to keep the cafe open. Or I guess I could open but I wouldn't have any coffee.

And if I didn't find my business partner, Shadow Joe, I wouldn't even have the lease on this place! But also, I know plenty of times I've tried to keep to a tight schedule, and it just keeps me from enjoying life—taking a trip somewhere neat, experimenting at the espresso bar, or even just getting ice cream at Echo Park Lake after a long day.

I mean, take that with a grain of salt because I sort of believe in the meaningless chaos of the universe and the impermanence of things. Maybe you've seen things I haven't? I'm just saying maybe sometimes what there is, is to sit down and really enjoy that moment instead of driving on to the next thing on your list.

Looking forward to our next chat, especially if you'll tell me more about going to Italy with your parents! That sounded fun.

[Natalie Lavigne]

Thank you, sir. Very wise. Lots to think about.

Grendma

[Mayumi Ikazaki]

Look some of you have these great Grendmas and you go visit them and they cook so many things for you and they play video games with you, and they like, tell you about the good old days. Well, my Grendma doesn't act like that. She's confusing and she scares me. When the parents have had it and need a reprieve from the three of us, we have to go to Grendma's, and it is in no way a picnic.

    I don't wanna hear about your stunning Grendma gifts and the picture of her from her wedding day to Grentpa and how she looked just like you at that age. I'm sick of it. Go jump in the reservoir. Or maybe come with me to my Grendma's place in that rickety old house on the side of the hill and, like, have to fight your way through her karate students and trick her front door so it lets you in without giving it any secrets and then sit there in her weird house with the candles and no internet while she tells you what to do about that boy you like or how to see through the Shadow Veil.

    Maybe I don't want to know what Leo dreams about, Grendma. Leave it alone.

Grendma

[Sam Mitchmoon]

Grendma?

[Mayumi Ikazaki]

Dad said it was time to visit Grendma and I got out of it by saying I had to study at Bandito's.
    Edit: Bandido's.

[Mayumi Ikazaki]

Fun fact: if you've got the mind juice, you can just make someone <u>think</u> you went on a date and then you don't have to. You can even imply it went bad so they will stop asking and finally go out with Katherine, who is honestly a better match.
    Ugh. Grendma called (on the phone?!) and she wants me to come visit.
    Maybe I will tell her I have a date after all?

[Corey Yuiop]

You know, what I wanna know is why Mayumi keeps spelling grandma 'grendma'.

[Mayumi Ikazaki]

That's how you spell it. G-R-E-N-D-m-a
    The caps are because of the emphasis on that syllable.

[Camel Riboy]

Mayumi!

[Mayumi Ikazaki]

What

[Corey Yuiop]

Who wants to tell her?

[Camel Riboy]

AaaaAAAAaa! ;)
    (I am making the correct vowel noise)

[Mayumi Ikazaki]

Since you're all apparently trying to get under my skin, I want you to know that Grendma and I have had a "reckoning" and now we get along brilliantly. No longer will I have to go and bargain with the front door to leave without announcing my exit. I helped her with one of her "projects" and now she has the "Talisman," which I guess is a locket with a picture of Grentpa in it? If she wanted a nice picture, I know where the old photos box is in the attic. I'm sure I could've whipped something up.
    Grendma is pleased about the locket I think?

[Esmerelda]

What are we doing for spring break?

[Hyper Akeelah]

SPRING BREAK! I plum forgot.

Grendma

[Mayumi Ikazaki]

Now candles are not allowed in the house. I guess one of the karate students lit a cigarette outside and the lighter made a big fireball. Was it... a gas leak? The front door isn't talking.

[Corey Yuiop]

Anyone down for a visit to the Gr<u>e</u>nd Canyon? ;)

[Mayumi Ikazaki]

Big news! For spring break, I will be spending the whole week with Grendma at her beach house!

Grentpa built it before the war but then they lost it (internment camps) and Grendma has been toiling "since the world was young" to get it back. And it finally happened. She said it will be a fixer-upper and so she uprooted herself last night without warning. I found the handwritten note in her normal spot on the porch, damp from the nighttime sprinklers. There was a liveliness to her scrawl that I haven't seen before. Grendma is a solitary creature of habit, keeping to her classes and projects. I guess I still don't understand what it is that she does or why strangers always show up at the front door, harried and world weary, ready to learn martial arts. Maybe it doesn't matter.

It's weird how someone can change in your mind after a conversation. I don't mean a thoughtwipe or mindblast, just... talking.

[Mayumi Ikazaki]

The beach house is really something. It's a vibe even before you step into the front door.

    I knew Grentpa built the house on the side of the hill in Echo Park also, but I didn't know the beach house was the exact same house design, except up on stilts. It was really something, after that long drive in Grendma's station wagon to round a lone half-grass, half-sand hill and to see a flat, empty beach spread out before us, the ocean the same shimmering golden color as the sand, which was the same color of the afternoon sun. And there in the middle of this blinding yellow expanse, that cozy familiar house silhouette. Up on stilts.

    A lone gravel road snaked around the hill and went most of the way to the stairs. Sparse little spikes of gray grass held the ground together where the wagon parked. While the driver got Grendma out of the back seat, I wandered out onto the beach proper. The top might be dry, but my sandal prints left little puddles and there was a *schlorp* sound when I picked my feet up.

    Oh, Grendma needs something, I'll talk about the house later.

Grendma

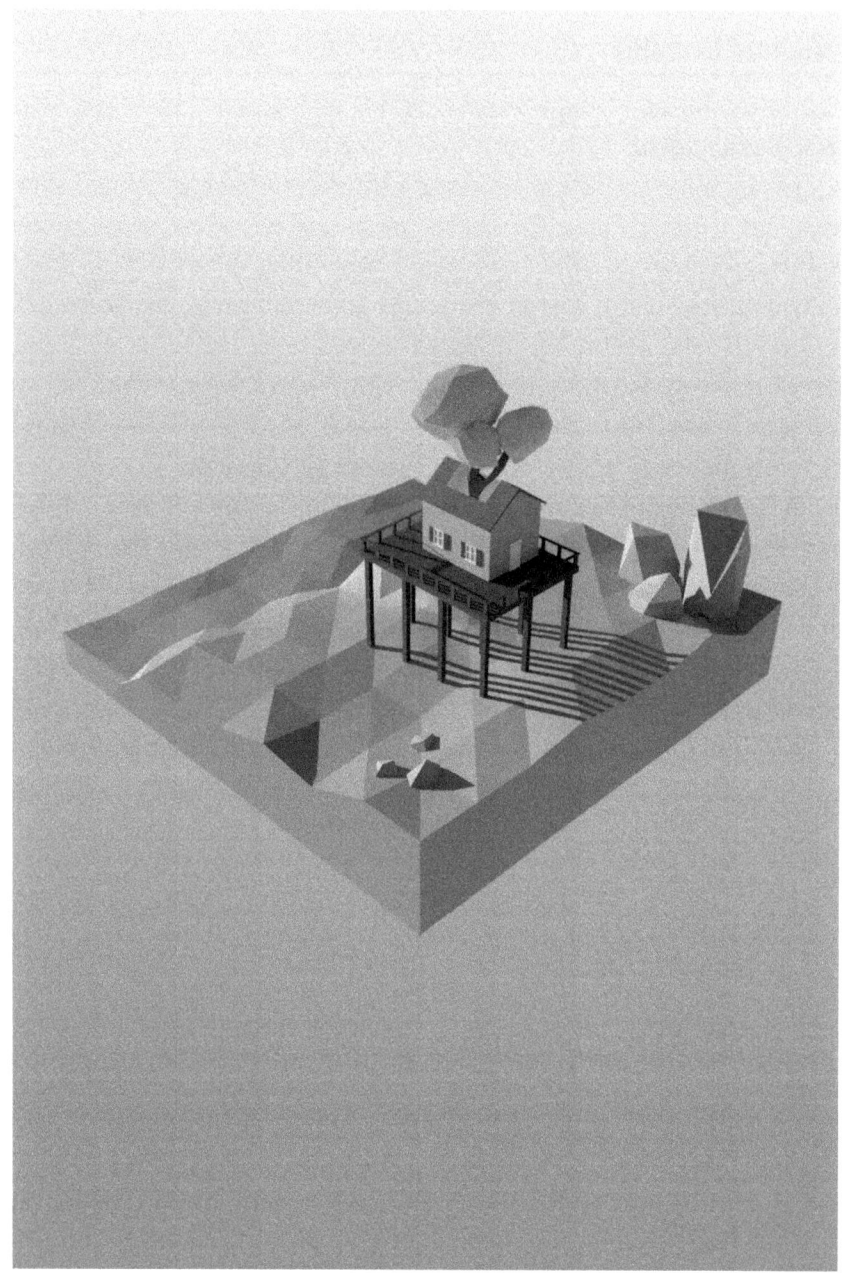

[Mayumi Ikazaki]

It's night and I can hear the crashing of waves and the wind against the sides of the beach house. Grendma is up still, chattering to herself about something as she shuffles around. I think she went outside a couple of times. She's so animated, got that pep or whatever.

I don't think I expected the ocean to be so noisy. That sounds dumb when I type it.

[Mayumi Ikazaki]

Last night, the wind and the waves crashed against the beach house again, and I couldn't sleep. I couldn't hear Grendma's chatter and shuffling, so I got out of my bunk and walked with bare feet on the vinyl floor into the living room with the big hole in the middle so Grendma can get her roots down into the wet sand for moisture. But she was gone, and the opening just looked straight down at sand lit green-gray in the moonlight.

I went out to the deck facing the ocean and pushed open the screen door. Down below, I saw Grendma in the dark surf, towering over waves that rushed in and around her roots. It was high tide, so the waves came to within a couple of meters from the stilts. And the beach between Grendma and the house was filled with a crowd of glowing green transparent people. They all stood rapt in a circle. I went to the rail and put a tentative hand out to reduce the risk of old house splinters. If I stood on tiptoes and leaned, I could just make it out. There were two ghosts in uwagis in the middle of the circle and they were kicking each other! Then one went down and Grendma screeched, and the next pair stepped into the circle, bowed, and started punching.

I think Grendma is here to hold some kind of fight tournament for ghosts.

Grendma

[Mayumi Ikazaki]

Today Grendma and I went kayaking and then laid in hammocks and read. No notes. A+.

[Mayumi Ikazaki]

Okay, the fight ghosts are back. Tonight, they are doing some kind of two-versus-two tag battle on the beach. I just saw a big, huge ghost pick another ghost up and legit yeet them into the ocean.

    Grendma looked over at the house while I was watching, and I had to duck out of sight. We've come a long way, Grendma and I, but I got a whiff of the old version for a minute there and it was very much not okay. To be stuck here in the middle of nowhere in a house on stilts with a hole in the middle, surrounded by warrior ghosts…

    Definite low point of the vacation.

[Mayumi Ikazaki]

Just one day left in this serene stay at Grentpa's beach house. Grendma is hopping around like she's a hundred years younger. And her branches have gotten stronger, from the salt water I guess.

    Today I learned she knows I've seen her at night with her "retreat." There was another reckoning (these are sparring matches, BTW. I have to fight her to resolve our differences) and we are good again.

    She says she learns from the old warrior ghosts to help her train her students, and they get a chance to socialize. It's a big fun annual event. She said she was sorry she hid this from me, that she was worried I wouldn't understand.

    I'm not the best at feelings and stuff, but honestly this whole revelation makes Grendma so cool. I didn't know how to react, so I just said all that. Then she placed a cluster of leaves on my shoulder, and I hugged her big wide trunk below her wizened bark face and stern brass eyes.

And she invited me to the big closing ceremony tonight. I'm going to go! Time to meet some ghosts.

[Corey Yuiop]

Mayumi! You can NOT leave it at that. What in the flip happened at the ceremony? Did you meet Brandon Lee in ghost form?

I'm sorry I teased you. I thought your Grendma was a grandma. Not a sentient fast tree.

(Fast because normal trees are too slow for karate.)

[Mayumi Ikazaki]

Yoooo. Back from Spring Break.

Ceremony was very fun, Corey, thank you very much. I did not meet a famous martial artist. I did get to shoulder throw a mongol though! The ghosts are solid, and they feel kind of like vinyl to the touch? Like a nice thick plastic sheet.

So, when it got dark, I could hear the ghosts chanting and when I went outside they were arranged in two audience blocks for the ceremony. Grendma was at the front facing them, and two of the fighter ghosts were facing each other in front of...

I think it was a wedding. Yeah now that I think about it, that's the only explanation.

Things might be weird at school, but I bet you haven't seen a ghost with fan blades and a ghost in a top hat with a sword cane get married.

Everyone was very happy and the party, if we're being honest, went on way too long. On the ride back we drove through a bunch of smoke from a fire and the smell got into the car air and it was not fun.

The end.

[Alexa Garcia]

I have taken to sneaking out at night to take walks.

 I lay there awake for a couple of hours staring at the ceiling, watching the rectangle the moon makes from my window crawl across the room. Without the constant regret and sadness of how I was before, there's just nothing there. Not in a bad way. It's honestly great. The only thing is I can't sleep. I'll be tired tomorrow. Again. And it'll be okay. Again.

 After a while of that, I feel bored and I kick quilt off legs and I sneaaaak into sneakers and I quietly push a psychic cushion under the window frame in the gutter thing where metal sits on metal, so when I slide it, it is so, so silent. And one leg is up and then the other and I am in the grass and the little metal hook on the gate goes up and I am in the night.

 It rained last night. It never rains. Curious.

 I pick a direction and start walking. Grandma would yell for an hour solid if she caught me. But I don't especially mind. The movement helps. Step, step, step and turn at the corner and it's a new street of houses and cars and palm trees black in the sky. Some streets don't even have streetlights. It's just dark and empty and quiet, except for the occasional skunk or coyote. If I were a housecat, it would be dangerous out. One of the mountain lions apparently got out into the neighborhood the other day, but I haven't seen him. Fellow traveler.

Sunset is down below. A fire truck flashes and blares on by. I keep going down a steep decline into the other part of the neighborhood.

I think I see Bianca.

Of course, it couldn't be her. It's after midnight and far away from her house. But in the moment I hesitate anyway. And go back the way I came.

My mind is blank. Heart beating away at an ordinary clip. So why would I do that?

A lone tree veers wildly in the air, like it's in a huge gust of wind.

Curious.

[Adult Lyle]

Alexa,

    It sounds like you're being super hard on yourself. Lighten up!

Love,

    Adult Lyle

[Alexa Garcia]

Hey, coffee guy.

    We've never actually talked, right?

[Adult Lyle]

Haven't we? Haven't we??? ;)

Vulcan

[Mikey12]

I had a really weird dream. Like I was werewolfin' in the hood. Except I definitely didn't get out last night.

Let me explain. I now have multiple redundant security measures at home to ensure I don't get out into the cool night air and run into the hills and attack hikers or house parties or housecats. It's never happened and so I am happy to report I am still a pure werewolf. No kills, baby.

But last night I had a dream that I had gotten free, and it was awful. I ended up on one of the windy hillside streets that are really scary to drive on and I remember seeing a nice couple with a really cute fluffy dog. I looked at the moon and she said it was cool, so I picked up the dog and...

Well.

Now I own a new phone thanks to Mind Meld (a Geom Flixstep, if you must know). And honestly just knowing it's on its way does make me feel better, even though I was saving that money for my trip to haunted part of Carlsbad Caverns (no tour has made it out alive!).

That app is really doing well, huh?

Vulcan

[Alexa Garcia]

I'm crying and I don't know why.

Or rather, I'm not crying, but water is coming outta my eyes like I would be. I feel fine, I don't get it.

[Alexa Garcia]

Okay, something is definitely seriously wrong and not with the world around me. At least, not more than normal.

I haven't really spoken to anyone in three days. I can go on my phone, but I haven't spoken to anyone out loud. And people have talked to me. I just don't feel the need.

Except I do have things I want to say. There was a compliment for Monika, she had a neat, embroidered skirt. And I wanted to tell Torreflot that I liked the test questions. I wouldn't even have thought about it but that's an unusual thing to say to a teacher I think. Right?

And last night Grandma asked me point-blank how I've been, and I honestly just looked at my phone until she left in a huff. How weird! I always talk to her. I just don't feel like it.

I don't feel sad ever since the machine, but now I feel scared.

[Alexa Garcia] [private journal]

I know what it is.

I haven't been able to sleep the last couple of weeks. Not really sure why. I just felt anxious for some reason. And I figured that, since Anderton's machine had been so helpful before, maybe there was a way to use it to calm me down.

So, I grabbed my jacket and shoes and walked out to Sunset and it was probably around one in the morning, but I didn't feel tired. I walked by tents and the occasional car until I got to the office, and I could see Nick the security guard making rounds through the glass. I used newly perfected mind powers to jimmy the locks open on the garage door and went into the back hall while I could sense him wandering through the cubicle farms on the second floor. I went to the stairs and crept down into the basement where I knew one of the machines was.

The doors there have electronic locks, but it doesn't take much when you can feel the circuits to just interrupt the magnets that let the alarm know when the door is open. And a moment later, I'm in a concrete room, just me and one of the machines. I didn't notice this during the day, but the projector screen where the thoughts appear is actually glowing faintly. Like it was radioactive. Which I'm sure it's not, but, um... hopefully, it isn't.

I went to the platform with the two spheres and put my hands on them, and with all the willpower I could muster I just focused on my fear. I wanted so much just to get this feeling outside of me.

So, I really hammered it. Fear, fear, fear. Scared, scared, scared.

For some reason, in that moment, I thought of Bianca.

And the machine rumbled and did its thing, and then, crystal clear on the projector wall, was a mirror image of the room and I was there, facing back.

Except, well, it was the room from the first floor. I could see the little high windows along the back wall.

And the mirror image of me? She was sad.

That's right. Sad. Not scared!

That means that whatever this mirror image was, it was the same one

Vulcan

from the last time I used the machine. Like a copy. And she's still sad. And now I can't be sad, like there's a part of me the machine removed. And that part is on the other side of this wall.

I took my hands off the spheres and the image held, and I went to the wall and got really close to that mirror image of me. And she really did look like me. It was even weirder being up close next to her. It felt even more like looking in a mirror, but the mirror image didn't move with me, didn't blink with me.

"Are you real?" I said.

"Of course I'm real!" mirror-me said in a wounded voice I knew all too well.

I really, really wanted to run at that point, but I'm glad I stayed there, because of what she said next.

"Where are you?" mirror-me said.

I said I didn't understand.

Mirror-me wiped away tears with the palm of her hand, just like I do. "I'm in this place," she said, "but it's weird. I'm trapped in the neighborhood, and there's—hiccup—no way out across Sunset."

And then the part that really scared me.

"There's a lot of us here."

I closed the projection and left before Nick could find me. It's seriously lucky the security guards aren't also PS13 alums.

Okay, so maybe me just typing out the conversation might not make sense, and I'm shaking so the words coming out of my head are going way faster than I can type.

I think that copy of me is real. Like, it can think. It just can't be anything but sad. So, it's not a perfect copy, more of an imprint made by the machine, like all the old carbon sheets on the forms the school makes us fill out.

I think the copy is a part of me that the machine stripped out.

She isn't the only one!!?!?! Anderton has been making copies of other students? Other people!?!?!?!

I don't know what they're being used for, but it's got to be tied to Mind Meld, right?

Still scared.

[Alexa Garcia]

It gets worse.

The Vulcan office on Sunset is vacant now. No desks, no chairs, no Mind Meld vans covered in flashing LED screens to drive to investor events. And from what I could see, the carbon-making machines are gone. I even ran into Nick the security guy and he said his company didn't know they were leaving. They did it overnight... the night after I... well, may have seen something.

Remember that prophecy about Lurkett and me from back at the start of the year? It feels like a hundred years ago. I haven't thought about it in ages. I definitely feel like I'm not a hero. I don't know what to do.

[Mikey12]

Um, hey, Alexa. Long time! Listen, this whole thing is real weird. Do you need to talk? Or do you need help? I can flip over a compact car. Maybe a truck (smaller one).

[Damien Cross]

Alexa, I think you're onto something. The Matrix has been super weird lately. Even in the safer parts, the little clockwork messengers are really skittish, like something is up. A bunch of them are crowded into rooms nearer the gateway entrances, and several of the doorways in the maze have been sealed up. It's like something else moved into their space and kicked them out.

Maybe you don't need to be a hero alone. I want to help. It may not be much, but I'll do what I can.

[Alexa Garcia]

Hmm. Well, I mean...

[Alexa Garcia]

Okay, you two meet me at the library after school. Go, go, go.

[ANDERTON NEO]

My friends,

The interns may have noticed that we had to relocate our offices over by the school. I apologize for the lack of notice. That one is on me.

But you should feel proud! Mind Meld has seen the most successful launch in web store history. We have more downloads and more dollars per user than just about anyone but the IRS (that's a little entrepreneur joke). People all over the globe are benefitting from Mind Meld, and you're a part of that. We couldn't have done it without you.

And in addition to the extraordinarily written recommendation letters you are now receiving by a crimson-clad, mysterious bike courier, I know you'll find that your time with us has benefited you in other ways too. The world is tough, and it takes real discipline to separate the parts of you that don't push you forward in life and take away their power over you. For that, you have my admiration.

Welcome to your future.

-Anderton Neo-
-Receive the Universe's Wisdom-
-Mind Meld-

[Mikey12]

Hey, Anderton! I know you can see these posts. We know what's up and we're gonna blow this whole thing wide open. Like Bentwater! Give Alexa's carbon back! I un-sign my Mind Meld user agreement!

[Janelle Avagyan]

Uh, yeah! I unsign mine too. Take me off your list, Neo.

[Mikey 12]

Also bring back all the other carbons you took from students. Don't make me come over there!
    (I am a seven-foot tall werewolf)

[Alexa Garcia]

Uh, yeah! What Mikey said. Mikey the freshman.

[Mikey12]

AND the other carbons you might have from somewhere else!
    ???
    Seriously how many carbons did this guy get?

[ANDERTON NEO]

Well, I guess the mountain lion is out of the park. (Get it? That's a joke. I can't help it if I'm hilarious.)

Yes, some of you have noticed, Mind Meld is a sophisticated, brilliant app and a warehouse team of thousands spread o'er the world. But it's also got some secret sauce. It's the reason we're absolutely ripping into certain other retail and online outlets.

It's your souls!

That's a joke again. It's not actually your souls. It's something much less valuable.

It's those wretched, useless moments of human weakness inside you. Excised and too far away to get their claws back into you. To pull you back from a sunny beach day to a good car cry punctuated by punching a streetlamp. It's the part of you you always wished you could pluck out with a pair of tweezers and put in a jar. I put em to work making people happy! Finally, that paranoia that keeps you glued to the wall at the dance has some real use, and you can cut a rug.

You're welcome.

-Anderton Neo-
-Receive the Universe's Wisdom-
-Mind Meld-

[Mayumi Ikazaki]

I log in on a Saturday to check what homework I missed, and the tech bro is on here like a cartoon villain yelling about how he's using carbons to manipulate people into buying on his stupid app. Cool.

Teachers check this thing on weekends right?

[ANDERTON NEO]

Nice, I was about to log off and order some halal food and lo, someone has graced me with their hot take.

No, whoever you are, it isn't manipulation. I'm not doing anything to you. And I don't hook them up to Mapquest and have the carbons go after Liz Lorde of 123 boring avenue. Carbons just do this. They just radiate their weak little hurt feelings out over the cosmos through those gates in the Matrix (the Internet) and it. Just. Works.

But you know what is nice? What I did.

You don't feel those dark little sad dejected feelings, amplified in your head. Because they're outta there. They're at Vulcan in a safe place where they can't tell you that you'll always be alone, and people hate you or whatever it is that your carbon whispers into your head.

I've given you the gift I gave myself all those years ago. And a thank you would be appreciated.

Okay bye.

-Anderton Neo-
-Get Over Yourselves-
-Mind Meld-

[Cole Abrams]

Wait, is he seriously saying he's using the carbons to make people... do what? Feel negative emotions and try to fix it by shopping?

[Mikey12]

Hey, Anderton! How dare you use my classmates' bad feels to control people! Those are for them to use, to make bad choices!

I'm throwing my Flixstep in the trash!

Or hmm. I am returning my Geom Flixstep! Give me an RMA number Anderton! No store credit! Put it back on my dad's credit card!

[Natalie Lavigne]

Nothing makes you want to buy junk like a feeling of loneliness, or anger. Or sadness.

Hmm. Makes me glad at least that I don't need things like that.

[Cole Abrams]

If only they sold attention on the app.

[Natalie Lavigne]

Well, I was going to wax romantic about how nice it is to be going back and forth with you on here, but never mind.

[Kelli Konrath, CEED]

What a weekend to take a camping trip.

I'm in touch with CEED and local authorities. Doctor M has been notified and is sailing back from Catalina right now in his communal trimaran, and the Paranormal School System superintendent is on her way.

Students, it's so important that you do not go after Vulcan. No matter how many plucky teen detective adventure stories you've read. Or how much tae kwon do you know.

TKD is for punching people off of horseback! These people are motivated by money. They are dangerous.

[Damien Cross]

I don't talk about it much, but I know what happened to Uncle Dill. Even if we don't officially actually know.

It was the luck.

A lucksmith is really lucky. That's how you can find exactly what you need or land a clutch hand grab over a leapt chasm.

But when your Big Moment comes... well, that's it. No scheme or skill or whatever will save you when your luck runs out in the service of whatever it is that makes us this way in the first place.

Dill knew. It made him fun and breezy and confident seeming because he was always determined to get the most out of every moment he had. That's what my mom and dad told me, anyway.

It scares me, but I think my big moment is here.

That seems really unfair, but lots of things are unfair. Or I guess they just <u>are,</u> and we call them unfair. It's unfair to call this curse lucksmith when I don't make it. It just is.

But still, if the moment can help people, maybe I can take the is-ness of it and make it matter.

A phone call? Who calls? Message!

Gotta go.

[Alexa Garcia]

Wow. This is happening. Here we go, I guess.

[ANDERTON NEO]

Oh, so Doctor M won't return my Facetimes but this login on this decrepit old website still works? Alright, I'll say what I need to say here.

I want you to stop. Whoever it is that's coming after me and Mind Meld should back off. You signed the paperwork. It's legally binding. You can't just come into my office and get into my life's work and muck it up. Not that you could if you wanted to! My home is a fortress!

I didn't do anything to you. But I promise if you keep it up, I will!

Alexa. The other ones. Please. You're bigger than this. Think of all the people you're denying happiness to.

And yes, this is cheesy as hell, but think of me. I listened to you! I did you a favor, and you've repaid me with sabotage and self-righteous anger.

Maybe that's the aspect we should've plucked out.

-Anderton Neo-
-Stop Being Petulant Children-
-Mind Meld-

Vulcan

[Cole Abrams] [personal log]

Back.

I... hmm.

I just crumpled up the SFS report I was filling out. This can't go in a report. But it should go...somewhere! So, I am writing it down.

I didn't think I'd be using this journal this much this year. A secretly on-point gift, thank you Mel and Malia.

Vulcan was gone from their office on Sunset, but it didn't take too many peeks (thanks also to Annabelle) to see that the machines were moved over to another building in Mid-City.

So, after actually not that much pleading, Harry got his old work truck and we went around and picked up Alexa, those freshmen guys, and after some deliberation on my part, I ended up asking him to get Nat, also.

I've never been so angry at someone who had to sit on my lap. Should have used that Metro ride share van.

A bunch of red-clad bike couriers tried to stop us at the truck loading dock, but I put them up in bubbles where their bike chains couldn't hurt us and they just flailed at the air, like useless red ninjas. They just yelled. Their faces red in the glow from LED-covered Jeeps. Nat zapped the security doors and fried the interior security system in textbook-perfect form. Like she does.

The inside of that place was so boring. It was all beanbag chairs and snack bars (many kinds of breakfast cereal, ready to go!) and plants and big wall windows.

Paranormal School 13

There was plenty to deal with. Even Alexa pitched in. She's gotten extremely vivid at her projections. Those tech bros had no idea they weren't looking at a projection of Anderton. Or that they were pitching startup ideas to said illusion for a solid eight minutes.

More than enough time for Nat and me to do our thing. Just like old times. We got into the first couple of security doors and made our way to the high-security wing which was much more my speed—gray sci-fi hallways with laser security fields. Just like in the SFS training videos!

So, we found the carbon projector devices (five of them?!), cut the power to the thingy while the portal was open, and just like Annabelle said would happen, the portals stayed open. And those carbons just shuffled through, and shuffled through, and shuffled through. They're all wandering around on Melrose right now. I guess the news and police showed up. CEED will have their hands full. How do you even get one of those things back merged with its person??

One snag, though. Alexa's carbon got away. And it's really the one I wish hadn't.

I don't understand how. And I don't understand why hers was such a terror. I might be a psychic, but that thing is on a whole other level.

Psychic power amplifies with clarity. Not just a clear mind, it took me a long time to learn that. Clarity of focus around an emotion—negative, positive, whatever. If you want an idea to be true enough… it can cut like a knife. If you have the brain for it.

Apparently Damien found her first, when we were all separated and wading through carbons.

The Alexacarbon started emanating these big bursts of psychic sob-waves and when we went towards the bursts, they stopped. Then started again farther away. Raw, shocking bursts of intense desperate sadness hit us in waves and tore gashes in the

Vulcan

walls and floor and shook the whole building and good grief it was hard to hold ground against that intense misery.

Damien was on the ground when we found him. Eyes open and blank. Looked like he'd taken a couple of those bursts point blank, trying to stop her.

Should've been me. I could take it. Maybe.

Nat zipped him to an ambulance. Not sure how he's doing but there was nothing coming from him, no pulse, no thoughts, not even the pulse from the nervous system tickling his brain.

So, the ride back (again, thanks Harry, an absolutely decent human) was a tad morose. Nat had her own seat at least.

[Alexa Garcia]

So.

Uh, I guess we saved the day. Except my carbon is gone. And I have no idea where. And she really hurt Damien, maybe killed him. And maybe condemned a building. The structural engineers guild is apparently over there now.

And... is it weird I'm worried about her like I was worried about Monika?

She's so strong. My carbon is, I mean. And in that moment in the lobby, she even looked over at me and it was like I was the reason she was sad. And then the sad turned into a burst of what looked like waves, like from the ocean! Knocked me on my butt. Crazy strong energy. Completely crushed an artisanal water bottle refrigerator.

And she blipped the flip up and left. Not through a door, I can only imagine. The moon? Do carbons need what we need? Do they breathe? Do they like... I dunno, hugs?

I—

Hang on. Wait.

What?!

[Alexa Garcia]

Okay, some context.

After we escaped Vulcan HQ and things weren't going anywhere, I got back home. I wasn't sure what to do next.

And...

Okay, so you know that weird bus that just appears and vanishes from the bus circle?

It was WAITING FOR ME OUT FRONT.

I am on the Moonside Bus.

The bus
was out front
of my house
waiting for me

with the little red stoplight signs popped out and flashing.

It wanted me to go with it. I could just tell.

I have no idea where it is taking me but I'm live blogging this madness.

[Alexa Garcia]

Still stuck on the bus. There's nothing outside the windows. It's just gray void. That sounds terrifying even by all this. *Motions around, and at the school year calendar*

Seems like it's going to take a while longer to get me to myself.

Ugh. Here we go. Might as well get it all out.

I like spending time with boys because at least they seem uncomplicated, and I don't have to worry as much about screwing things up. And this all started when that got proven right again.

Bianca and I were at the open mic that happens up Sunset at the little lounge coffee place. The one that now I guess all the PS13 students have found and won't shut up about? Joke's on them. The normal kids found that spot and have been going for a while.

So, we were there and Bianca had a scheme. She and some other friends (Nathan!) had been pestering me about performing a poem at this open mic for months. And I didn't know and I should have known, but they put my name in when they saw I had my notebook with me.

Bianca is the kind of person who will force you to do something because she knows it's good for you, and then get mad at you if you're mad at her for being so hardcore.

Anyway, so the last kid gets down and the host lady reads my name and I'm getting pushed up there by Bianca and she smiles. Her big gold hoop earrings are glinting in the stage lights and I say, "Okay, fine."

And I pull out my notebook and I go up to the wooden stool and set it on there and my hands are shaking as I flip it open and find the poem.

It was the one about the blue cat.

And I read. And everyone was quiet, and I was just looking at the sheet and worrying about how close I was holding the mic and whether I should stop or not.

What I didn't know was that I was using my powers without realizing it the whole time.

As I read a bit from the poem, stuff would appear in the air around everyone. There was a little bus stop, the lady with the bike, and that cat showed up. (These are things from the poem.)

By the time I got to the end, the air was full of little glowing things, exactly as the parts of the poem appear in my head when I think about it. And I looked up and I was obviously horrified because everyone was horrified at what was going on, staring at these little glowing things that shouldn't exist. I know now I was projecting all this stuff automatically as I was picturing it.

And then I saw Bianca in the front row and...

Okay, I should step back. Since I'm telling this whole thing now, I should explain.

Bianca and I... I mean... I don't think I like girls. Or what am I saying? Obviously I do. We were friends first, but we definitely kissed one time. Like a real kiss.

It was my first kiss if we're being honest. Ugh.

And when I saw her up above us in the room, a projected me and a projected Bianca floated in the air, leaned in, and—

Even typing that makes me horribly, miserably embarrassed. Looks like the carbon didn't take embarrassed with it, just sad.

That was about it for me. I grabbed my stuff and went for the door and when I got outside Bianca followed me and she was super angry. And I said I was sorry, but she just kept yelling. And she was right. What I did was embarrassing for her. We hadn't told anybody! And now half the school knew. And I got super upset.

The really messed up thing is I think about that moment now, and I remember how hurt I felt. Like, my best friend yelling at me for betraying her trust. And she was right! I did. But I didn't know how it had happened or what would happen next. I didn't do it on purpose! I just knew my friendship was over and I wanted to curl up in a ball under the old lemon tree in my back yard and never talk to anyone ever again.

But now? I can remember crying, but instead of the feeling of hurt, I just feel... the physical feeling of my chest going up and down with the sobs and tears going down my cheeks. But I don't feel sad.

Am I broken forever? Can I be fixed? What if I can't? What if my carbon does something else? Something worse?

[Alexa Garcia]

Okay, so it's the last chance to post something, says the bus.

Not the bus, I guess it's the driver. Normally, the bus looks like the driver's seat is empty. That's how it always looked when I walked by it. But it isn't. Or is it? I don't know. I am sworn to secrecy.

Outside is a kaleidoscope of light and color, strands of blue and gold light stretch between shimmering other worlds and times. We're hurtling, like the bus got thrown like a football.

I can see why people are afraid of this thing. It's like the old candy movie on TV.

Uh, it's hard to think and hard to type because my hands are shaking. And I really want to type a last thing, but I can't think.

...

[Sarah Cartwright]

Paranormal School 13
Mandatory Student Journal Contact Sheet (Pink Copy)
Date: [March 28, 1994]

I saw the big fight that happened over La Brea. I saw it all and it was crazy! I am still frightened.

Or I guess I heard it first. Grace and I were shopping for chic, vintage hats in American Rag and there was a huge thunder roar outside. I ran out, still wearing a wide-brimmed hat like Blossom would wear and I looked up and a blast of wind hit us, and we looked up into the afternoon sun. High above the intersection in the biggest psychic aura I'd ever seen was a tall-ish, slender silhouette contorted into a hunched pose.

And she shuddered, like a sob, and it was amplified and mind-bendy and the sky changed color and every window on the street burst out. People were running and screaming, and I saw a couple of people just lying there. It was obvious she was some kind of psychic entity, but I had no idea what we were supposed to do to stop her.

Grace threw up a barrier and did some beams, but the shadow just shrugged them off. Never saw something get the best of Grace like that. It was like a puppy trying to fight the Ultimate Warrior.

And right when Grace's barrier cracked, there was a big, loud HONK from up the street and a yellow school bus was just there, where there hadn't been anything, and a tall-ish, slender girl with long brown hair climbed out and went towards the entity.

And the shadow up in the air started throwing some serious stuff at her. Golden and blue waves of psychic energy that cracked the street and crunched into cars. But the tall girl just let them pass over her and kept walking. It was like the she was phased out of solid reality.

And then the girl looked so determined, and she closed her eyes. I felt energy fold on the street surface, and she silently leapt up to the shadow.

Vulcan

They hovered there in the air, circling, for a long time, as the power lines buzzed and rattled in the wind and the sirens converged from everywhere. And then, instead of a big fight, the girl opened her arms and embraced the shadow. And there was a flash, and they sort of swam over each other and then there was just one person—the girl—falling towards the street.

I'm not sure, but I think I heard the hero girl say the other one's name. It was "Lurkett." Does this mean we get to add a Titan to the database? Can I give her a first name? Serpentina?

Grace had the forethought to catch the new unified girl with a crash bubble. That's why she's in Students for Safety and I sit around not doing my English reading. And she caught the girl and before the cops could do anything, we'd blipped out and were back in the 500 building and a bunch of CEED people just *vooped* in from space and they took the girl away.

They were going to wipe our memories, so I guess it was something serious. But I said I'd write about it in my journal, so they let me keep the memories. For the journal.

Who reads these anyway?

[Natalie Lavigne] [secret diary]

Millie,

It was a return to SFS days of old. I had wondered if perhaps such a thing was impossible with these constant spats with the ol' partner. Spats and... uh... occasional bursts of affection. Like living potions bubbling up unexpectedly in a cauldron beyond my power to make a mess of things. It's been another book stacked high in the proverbial backpack.

But would I be lying if I said it wasn't nice to know that if I text, he texts back? Yes, alas. Even if it's to argue, the reliability of it is...

So, Cole texts on the weekend. And suddenly, I am sitting on his lap in a truck and we're on our way to the headquarters of the world's biggest shopping tech company. And I got the sense (just a guess, none of those psychic reads happening in this head) that even though he was determined to help and even though he was glad I was there, he was still very annoyed with me. I think the giveaway was how he'd look away if we made eye contact. This lingering hint of something, and then a deliberate shove-off.

Sir, what is it?

And it was quite the crisis. I've seen some intense things in the last two years, but that didn't prepare me for an assault on a tech fortress to rescue an army of emoting psychic zombies led by a shockingly powerful Titan sad about the horrors of adolescence.

I also didn't expect to be attacked by the smart devices on my person. Headphones snaking, earbuds swarming like flies, phone like a little tough glass fist. It's enough to switch a girl back to decaf (and by decaf, I mean flip phones and CD players). Many questions were raised as to just what these gizmos can do, and what they know.

Hmm, I'm not sure anyone else even mentioned that part. There was a lot going on.

The young lucksmith, Damien, is doing okay. I zipped him to an ambulance and as they were strapping him to the gurney, he came to groggily. He gave me this little smile and said, "I guess it wasn't."

Whatever that means.

I have to admit I can relate to this specific Titan. Millie, what young woman doesn't emanate sadness that feels mighty enough to topple bridges? Especially when the report card arrives at home. I'm sure more than a few would say yes to that kind of manifestation of power, even if it went ruin around them.

Something nice is owed in return for this adventure. After all, Cole was the one with the olive branch. And I promise I don't do this on purpose, but I get the impression I can compartmentalize.

Oh, I think I know what I could do.

[Mikey12]

I got shot with a sadness blast and it turned me back into a human. I HATE it! I'm so small and naked! It's so cold and I can't slam stuff. How do any of you do this?! Augh!

[Ebit Nicole]

TRANSCRIPT OF MORNING ANNOUNCEMENTS FOR MONDAY, MAY 1

Good morning PS13! This is Ebit Nicole and Don Chang. Reunited now and forever (until June 15).
 The weather today is sunny and cool. Temperature will be sixty-four degrees.
 Lunch today is Turkey Blitz. Thanks to recent state legislation, the Blitz is now able to be enjoyed without a permission slip. Wear a bib!
 This day in Paranormal School System history: Did you know that Anderton Neo is missing? After the incident at Vulcan HQ, various Vulcan employees have reached out to PS13 staff to ask if perhaps they have seen him.
 Vulcan is currently under investigation from multiple paranormal and normie entities and attempts to use the Mind Meld app cause an error popup reporting the service is "in review."

Apparently, the only report of an Anderton sighting is a PS13 senior Remote Viewing student. The student reported a vision of a thin, terrified, sunglasses-clad man running from what appeared to be his equally frightened twin off of Abbot Kinney in Venice.

Critical Announcement: Students who gave up a carbon to the tech company Vulcan, please come re-merge with your carbon in the basketball gym. Unclaimed carbons will result in involving parents and guardians, and I think we can all agree this one is better left at PS13.

[Pause, Ebit listens to someone off camera]

Scratch that! The school's official policy is parents and guardians have complete transparency into the educational process and disruptions at schools in the Paranormal School System.

Normal Announcements: The Chess Men club will be renamed to Chess, Man! and begin accepting all members from everywhere. Please experience chess! Now, while there is still time.

Graduation is just around the corner! Make sure you invite your friends and family to be there on your big day! Seniors only. All other graduates have to come back next year and do not get a ceremony.

That is all. Have a safe, productive day, Paranormal School!

[Cole Abrams]

I know I sound like a broken record, but my stepdad is an impressive guy. I know you're not supposed to like your stepdad, but Harry is the real deal. And it didn't start with the very appreciated ride to save the world (universe?) during the Mind Meld incident. He has always been just utterly decent and cool.

When I get home some days, I try to take two or three of the little sisters off his hands for a bit. He always looks tired. I have enough trouble with two of them running around. Sometimes he's got little fingerprint handprints on him from paint or dirt or whatever, but he never seems to mind.

I wonder sometimes if they've got the gift like I do. And will they just be normal psychics or will they end up with crazy telekinetic emotion powers? I don't know what Harry would do if they could get up into a cupboard and then throw up a barrier.

Or worse, imagine five psychic teenage girls fighting. They'd take the roof off the house.

Okay, that's a little scary. I'm gonna go do some homework.

[Alexa Garcia]

You don't have to be afraid of your carbon.

I know lots of you must be freaking out with these things coming home looking just like you.

Here's what I did with mine. After we broke the Mind Meld generator in the Vulcan HQ, all the carbons were set free, like they were released from a spell, and I ran down a long hallway of confused looking colorless miserable faces until I found mine. And yeah, like Cole said, she flipped out and attacked us and got away.

And some other stuff happened. A LOT of other stuff but I'm trying to teach everyone about carbons so let's just skip to the part where I'm in the air with her in 1994.

...hmm.

It was weird. I don't... I guess when it's me doing the sad feels, I get mad at myself. But looking at my carbon and how hurt she was... well, I don't know. It felt different. I felt more understanding. But also, I knew it would be okay in a way I never did before when I was sad. It was like I was my own friend. There to comfort her. Shower her with love I'd never have shown myself when all this was just happening inside me.

Meanwhile, my carbon is going on this sob-rant, and it's all stuck specifically around the open mic with Bianca. She's like a broken record. She just keeps saying, "That stupid blue cat! That stupid blue cat!"

And I held my hands out in the bright sun, and the carbon put its arms around me and pressed its face into my shoulder. And of all the truly bizarre things I've seen this year, holding myself while she sobbed is definitely the top of the list, by far. And then, the sadness and loneliness were back. I felt what she felt running away from the dance. The first day or two at this school. Even the way my little brother yells at me to get out of the living room when his friends are over.

And Bianca, face red with fury and embarrassment, telling me I was a liar and an asshole out on the sidewalk at night in front of the cafe. That I was a bad friend and a creep, and she hated me. And the part after when I was sitting on the little wall in front of my grandma's house in the dark and everything felt completely wrong in the world.

I'd forgotten about that last part. I sat there listening to this really old band, Zero 7, for at least an hour. As the cars drove by.

At some point I realized I wasn't holding my carbon anymore. I was just floating up there, actually crying this time. Tears and sobs working normally, sir. Yes, sir, much crying.

And I actually, really felt better then.

Then I passed out and woke up back here. Uh, again, skipping some stuff.

So, you see, you don't have to be afraid of your carbon. It's just part of you, coming home.

[Cole Abrams]

I woke up again in the Unknowable classroom, with its blank walls and windows looking out over a foggy mountaintop expanse that is always orange with sunset light.

I'm not sure what I've learned but I guess the class is over now because my final grade is on the website.

I don't think I deserve an S. An A or a B would be fine, I didn't do anything and I for sure didn't learn anything.

[Xenton X]

Cole! This is so unfair. I still haven't been to the class, and I've tried everything. No one has been to class but you, they can't fail us for that!

[Damien Cross]

I got to the class, too, while I was in bed at the hospital recovering. I went to sleep with my broken leg up in its big white cast, and when I opened my eyes I was stuck to a light gray wall like I was a spider-powered hero. Down below in a rectangle of red-orange light from the window was a teacher's desk with a little cup of pencils and an old beige computer monitor. And the guy at the desk looked up at me with kind eyes that looked sort of familiar, gave me a thumbs up, and grabbed a key ring out of a brown metal desk drawer.

The mystery teacher left. I crawled around on the walls for a while, and then bam! Back in the hospital. Cool.

Big familiar energy from the teacher. Big familiar. Like, teacher's aren't that nice. I'm sure I could go crazy guessing what was going on but the parents brought my Nintendo, so I've got other stuff to do (play Fortnite).

[Rodney Gemini (Moon Facet)]

My family planned this big weekend trip to a popular regional theme park destination and when I got onto a roller coaster and they clicked the bar shut, I was suddenly in an old metal desk in a blank gray room with bright orange sun shooting through the windows.
    The Unknowable class! It finally happened!
    I hung out in the classroom and the teacher stood up and he gave this long-winded speech about how I was gonna learn a ton of things from the class, and then got a notification on his phone and got some keys out of the desk and ran out of the room.
    I couldn't open the door, so I spent some time using the desk like a club to slam windows and stuff. I came to in the car on the drive back from the regional theme park. I know it was real because my twin was extra sunburned, but I was not!

[Rodney Gemini (Moon Facet)]

I GOT MY GRADE! IT'S AN S!

[Xenton X]

Uh, still no grade here. Hello? You don't understand, PS13 Admin, my parents aren't cool enough to allow a grade gap! I can't just tell them, "I got assigned a mystery class you can't get to" and have that be it.
    If the conversation goes on too long, I just know I'm going to panic and spill the beans about something, like using the portal in the 300 building bathroom to warp to Nigeria for a couple days.
    You don't know what you're doing to me, school!

The Invitation

[Natalie Lavigne]

I keep having these memories of a dinner with my parents that didn't happen.

We are sitting at our big dinner table in the formal dining room, but we never use that space. We have kitchen dinners at the round table next to the granite kitchen island, with the windows looking out over the pool and a green hill of houses that twinkle with lights.

But no. Tonight we're in the formal dining room and there's only the two narrow windows with sheer curtains blocking a view of the driveway and the dirt side of our hill.

The parents are at either side of the chair at the head of the table, facing each other, and I am to Mom's left in the second chair down. When I picture it, I remember her scolding me for some manners thing, which is normal. I must have done something several times because I can feel her grab my wrist, dozens of her silver metal bracelets pressed between our arms.

The rest of the house is dark, like it is when the parents are away. I can make out the staircase and the front door and the study next to it. The way to the living room is dark, but the TV over the mantle is glowing.

The Invitation

I excused myself, took my plate (empty! No food!) to the kitchen and walked to the TV glowing in the dark. I said this before. This is very unusual. The living room is always lit up. Ready to entertain guests. Hypothetical guests.

And just looking at the TV, I remember I felt deeply nervous. Something was way, way wrong with it.

Hang on, I'm getting a text. Computer friend, we will chat later.

[Natalie Lavigne]

Okay, that was Annabelle, and she wishes to talk my SAT prep. Third time 'round, thank you very much, parents.

Back to this memory.

The dinner is more or less wrapped up and I clear the parents' places, and once the dishwasher is loaded, I head back into the living room, and the TV really is just on a blank white screen. It's super creepy. And when I'm in the living room, I can actually hear noise coming from it. Really subtle whispers. I can't make any of them out but it's creeping me out. And it gets crazier because I start walking towards the TV, but I don't want to. I'm not telling my legs to move. They're just moving.

And the TV is cold, for some reason. It's emanating cold like an industrial air conditioner. I can feel it brushing at my hair and cutting through my blouse.

Now I'm just a couple of steps from this thing, and whatever it is, it's not a TV. I can feel a whole world behind it, stretching out in every direction. All I see is white, like my eyes can't deal with it, but I can feel what's there.

My parents grab me and and pull me to the ground. The TV is a TV. The lights are on in the living room like it always is.

And then the most unnerving, most unlikely thing of all happens. My Mom hisses in my ear, "Never do that again."

And I wake up in a sweat.

Ugh, I'm late to meet Annabelle now.

[Cole Abrams]

They coaxed the seniors out to the gym today as a class, and in between whispered jokes from Quimby and Morgan, they managed to get across the schedule for the rest of the year. Classes, finals, but also the looming specter of graduation. The ceremony, the other stuff they're doing those last weeks of school, like the graduation lock-in and the Short Form Divination Entertainment Hour. It's a lot. SFS is even doing their own little thing, just for the seniors.

I think I'm excited about graduating. Right? There's college. I've got applications in at UCLA and Desert Moon Psychic Academy. Should hear back in the next couple of weeks. People are already getting their letters. And I'll get the summer and I won't have to ever wake up early in the morning to go to school or work ever again, maybe.

What else is going on? SFS has been weirdly quiet. People seem kinda… happy? Not actually happy, but it's almost like the fallout of the Mind Meld incident has calmed down the more chaotic elements at the school. Camila is somehow allowed out of the Maw, maybe due to a special agreement to make up classes? She wore a feather boa yesterday and she bared her fangs at me warmly. Not really her style previously. Was it the boa? She honestly looks good, considering.

Oh, she was one of the ones that split and reunited with a carbon. Maybe that's why she's chill now. I wonder what exactly her carbon's emotion was. Fury? Something a little more interesting?

Final assessment: Louis has been good as a partner. He doesn't make me read as much weird stuff as Natalie did. He also doesn't do enough homework, but that's not my problem.

I didn't even think of Natalie that much, except during the Mind Meld crisis the other day when it was almost automatic to bring her along. That instant "you" choice kind of freaked me out, but it was over eventually and then I was back to not thinking.

But then last night, I had a dream she invited me over.

"Hey, you should come over." Like she did a bunch of times over the past year.

And I was skeptical because there was always a reason it wouldn't

The Invitation

happen. Homework would come up as I was walking over, or some crisis with her family or she literally wouldn't answer the door. And I'd get angry and leave and we'd argue later.

Even now, she just comes outside and sits where I can see her, as if it's on purpose, until some obligation beckons and she runs off, lugging books.

But this time in the dream was different. I remember she grabbed my wrist in the dream. And I <u>felt</u> it. And she was wearing bracelets that jangled against my arm and she looked intently into my eyes and said, "I'm so excited to see you."

The mind is a weird, fickle thing.

[Cole Abrams]

Aaaaaand I just got a text from her inviting me over for dinner.

[Cole Abrams]

We haven't talked in weeks unless you count like fifty words during the Vulcan thing. What is going on?! For all the times I've been "invited over," not once has it been dinner related.

What are her parents even? Her mom is nice enough but it's like she's a face in a doorway. What does it all mean?

[Cole Abrams]

I've been thinking about the concept of Nat's dad and all I've settled on is there's probably a lot of tweed happening in their vicinity.

[Natalie Lavigne]

The truth is, I've never seen the parents' home so much and so adamant about having someone over. I am trepidatious. What do they have planned? Snacking and small talk outside next to the pool? A pointed interview at the kitchen island?

Lasagna??

The Invitation

[Cole Abrams]

So. Dinner.

I go up to the house above the reservoir and knock on the door and... honestly, I wanted to leave. I felt frustrated and weird, like I was in five different timelines at once and in every reality, I was doomed to forever be on this doorstep wondering if Nat was going to answer the door this time. Like that's how I'll be for the rest of my life. Just waiting for a yes? What am I doing? I'm an idiot.

And yet, there I was.

I hate that you can't delete what you type in this dumb website.

And then the door opens, and Nat's dad is there.

And again, I have *never* seen Nat's dad, but it's immediately obvious it's him. I was right about the tweed. He had a brown jacket on with the elbow patches, and a button-down green shirt. And he's got a mustache (soup catcher type, of course) and he gives me that weird old guy warm welcome like he's trying his best to be normal around someone he's never met. But no one is normal.

"Cole! It's so good to finally meet you. Come in!" That sort of glad-handing.

Sure, sure. I'm still thrown by how exactly he matches the Nat's dad in my head.

He steps aside so I can enter, and I walk into this spacious entryway with Nat's actual harp (!) sitting in a side room on the left, separated by windowed doors. Everything is cream-colored except for these dark, almost black, wooden floors. And the weirdness starts then because Dad isn't next to the door anymore. He's in the living room up ahead, past a carpeted staircase with bannisters that end in little spirals. He didn't flash or zap, like Nat does. He just wasn't and then he was. I noticed he was there and then he was. Like the Moonside bus I guess.

"Can I get you a drink? Whiskey sour? I'm just kidding. A soda? Tea? What do you like?"

Around my arrival to the kitchen island, I realize the furniture in the house is blinking, like he does. Here when I notice it but in the

The Invitation

corner of my view it suddenly isn't, and the living room is empty. I glance and the huge expensive leather couch is back.

Nat is in the kitchen with her mother, who still has her woosh of gray hair. She floats over and gives me this big hug. Her feet don't touch the ground, but she's pretty short, like Nat, so I'm still taller.

Okay, Dad blinks and Mom glides. I guess that's how Nat gets to a zip?

They're making dumplings, which I've never seen someone make, even though we get takeout dumplings all the time and I love them. Yum. This is promising.

Nat puts the spoonfuls of filling onto the little dumpling circles and gives me this smile that isn't quite right. I'm still so rocked by every little thing that I don't catch it. Not good.

Doctor just walked in. More after.

[Natalie Lavigne] [secret diary]

Millie,

It is a remarkable thing, what the parents are like with Cole. I didn't get it at first. They're so enthusiastic. So warm.

"So, son, how's your family?"

"I hear you got into the Unknowable class. And you passed it! Remarkable."

"You know, Natalie speaks so highly of you. The book monster story is one of my favorites. You make quite a team."

They're never like this with me.

Cole lights up and he looks at me with those kind brown eyes and he just emanates a raw electric affection that I have (at least partly) planted in him. Egged on by the parents with leading questions. The chickens have come to roost. We are to be awed by their command. I didn't expect this, but I see how I may have created the situation.

At least partly. Hah.

All I wanted was someone who would not deliver an edict, not command, not demand another achievement. Something special to distract.

The parents exchange a look with each other, a shared silent approval, and I just feel more and more wrong, but I can't remember why. It was like an echo of a warning from a dream version of me from a year ago, hollering, but faint and small.

Millie, Millie, Millie, Millie.

Who am I writing to? Who are you?

The Invitation

[Cole Abrams]

Bandages and stitches and shots. Favorite shirt ruined. More tests. Bright green hospital lights. A very worried mom, still in her scrubs. Don't worry, I already had the bruises.

From what, you ask?

Oh, I shouldn't talk about the Vulcan thing. She'd have a conniption.

"I got in a fight with JR."

[Natalie Lavigne] [secret diary]

You'll have to do, Millie, whoever you are because I have to write this down. In case I forget again.

The conversation at the fancy dinner table wanders its way past appetizers and salad to the entrees. Mom brings out the little round container and takes the lid off and we pluck dumplings out onto plates with chopsticks and stir soup to kick up the good stuff that had settled.

"So, Cole, tell me something."

This is how the questions come now. And they're deeper. Did he notice? That this had become an interrogation?

"Where do you see yourself in ten years?"

"How do you deal with stress?"

"What's important to you?" (He mentions his sisters.)

And then the parents sit silent, approving, while Cole talks and I eat. The parents' silverware taps and clinks on fine china around the little compartments of food on their plates. Not touching them. So as not to ruin the work.

Did he notice? That they do not eat?

Had I noticed?

It feels unnecessary to warn him, even though now it almost makes me a little ill to write it.

A new question pends. The eye contact comes intensely from mother, such that Cole pauses mid-bite, stuffs the half a dumpling in his cheek like a squirrel.

"Do you love our daughter?"

The parents wait, their turned heads form identical angles in a triangle.

Did he notice? That they do not breathe?

I see it now. How could I not know that?

Cole still has not chewed. In fact, the other half dumpling is pierced on his chopsticks, six inches from his mouth.

He manages a muffled, "What?"

That is somehow satisfactory to the parents, even though Cole is still frozen, a deer in big truck headlights.

Mother says, "You excel at so many things. You complement each other wonderfully. It seems like a pairing that should be, doesn't it? You just have to say you want to be with her."

And now Cole chews, swallows, and in the smallest, most honest voice he has ever used, he says, "I do."

And the parents peel back their hands and golden tendrils swarm at him.

The Invitation

[Cole Abrams]

I'll probably end up putting this in an SFS report at some point, on account of I hit the emergency button on my wristband when they shot golden claw beaks to attack me. One of them got the back of my hand, a real nasty gash that dripped these two big, round red dots onto the beige tablecloth.

It happened so fast it took me a half-second to process what was happening. These tendril things weren't beaks. They were little needles and scissors. Surgical tools. Or close enough.

Vague memories of some messed up children's book that scared the hell out of me when I was little. About a monster that sews little stuffed animal children together, to make quilts.

Why?

I still don't get it. But I jumped up. And I admit, aside from the instinct to jump back, I didn't do anything. This is so dumb, but it was like I didn't want the moment to end. Like even what those things were, what they really meant by *pairing*, I still wanted it to be the thing I'd always wanted.

It just seemed like such a good idea.

Natalie snapped out of it first.

[Natalie Lavigne] [secret diary]

Now they are less person-shaped, and the threads fill the entryway, and I throw my weight into Cole while he gawks and bleeds.

It's coming back to me easier now. I could see the moment I chose them. I could see the moment clearly. On the other side.

Where I am from... uh, how do I say this? Parents are... requisitioned? That's not quite it. The limits of curved marks on a 2-D plane to convey ideas.

He picks me up, out of the way of biting cutting tendrils as they block the entryway and encircle the living room, caking in corners, circling in on themselves.

In this limited place, I can truly expand forever. I just don't because that seems rude.

The parents do not understand rudeness. They are visitors here. They don't understand what a person is, in the human sense. The id, ego, superego. The need for occasional anime binges.

They just see what we are back home, and they want me to be more. To fill out the sculpture? That's not quite it either.

And I do want to be more. I had it all planned out. But apparently it wasn't enough.

Cole throws up a barrier and golden glowing lines ricochet. My partner is back!

[Cole Abrams]

And in that moment we were a team again. She leapt up, a solid twenty-four-inch vertical leap, zipped around behind the two of them, zapped against my barrier and the shockwave vibrated the mother such that she had to pull the tendrils back inside her human form and fell to the ground, shuddering. The dad lost control of his blinking and actually blinked halfway into the entryway wall with that gold framed antique mirror but was cogent enough to keep the tendrils coming.

I would normally react with horror at someone messing up parents that bad, but I made an exception.

Barrier cracked at points, the little tendrils ate at it, like my psychic energy was a grid of sandwich pockets. Deeply unsettling. A new layer of unsettling.

But Nat was there, standing ground with me. Lots of things might

The Invitation

or might not happen. But that moment was something I'll never forget. It was the absolute best to have her back.

Right, the fight. Tweed Dad and Rogue Mom had split up, to attack the barrier from different sides, and we were either going to have to bust through the ceiling (my preference) or a wall to get out.

But Nat hit my arm and pointed. The barrier had cut through the wall with the fireplace and the TV on it. And the TV was on. But like, weird on. No need to say anything. I knew the rules of this sort of fight. I grabbed and pulled, and the TV came off the wall, stayed on with no power and she took my hand and I let go of the screen. It fell towards us and we were in an indigo expanse with nothing for miles in every direction, spiraling as our own bodies spun open in a shower of golden threads that sailed out from us like jellyfish tentacles the length of train cars.

The TV screen opening/gate/portal/whatever it was, still sails "down" from us. The barrier broke when we left. The parents and their surgical tools are surging through the white opening, snaking out to this other place, but they're drifting away faster than they can get to us.

My vision shimmers a layered kaleidoscope, like viewing things through a bug's hundreds of eyes. I eventually realized it was because my eyes were made for three dimensions and this, whatever this space was, was more.

[Natalie Lavigne] [secret diary]

Millie, you're one of us, aren't you?

Never mind. I'll get around to it. Keep being you and hold still. I am not done.

Sometimes, when I would meet another student's parents, and they had big controlling energy, I would wonder. Are they from where I am from? Certainly, my parents are not the only ones of their kind. And they are not individuals in the way humans are. They are all of them, at once.

But they are also just automatons.

In that expanse, everything I need is there to reach for. It's an easy thing to close the book that is the portal through the TV, clip the parents sufficiently. Reach out to their source. This is instinctual now. Why I would hide this from myself? It doesn't make sense, but here we are. And I sever the contract.

The collective intuits it will send me an invoice for breaking the contract early.

I am free of so much.

Where do I take my confused friend? He is currently flailing in a way that will alter his future, possibly also the course of the earth.

(Through the cosmos, not through time.)

The Invitation

[Cole Abrams]

We touched down on carpet.

This was a shoeless house, and boy, was carpet texture a welcome feeling on my sock-covered toes.

She asked if I was okay.

The cut! I looked down. It had scabbed over. Something about the interdimensional jaunt we'd just taken.

In contrast with all that, Nat's bedroom was utterly normal. There's her huge laptop on a little blue desk in the corner. There's a tall dresser with curved wooden drawers, and a wall of pictures of friends above. She's got one of those beds with the posts that I can't remember the name of. There was a pile of clothes in the corner, unhampered.

I am disarmed.

Was I there on the wall of pictures? I looked closer. Yep, it's a little Instax print from Winterween, pinned to powder rose wall with a sunflower yellow thumbtack. We were smiling.

Hmm. And while I stood there awkwardly, next to the door and that black, empty hallway, she started to change.

She took off her earrings and put them in this felt box on her dresser. She slipped off her headband and mussed up her hair. She slipped off black slip-ons and tucked them into their cubby with her toes. They joined their shoe friends in their little rack next to the closet. I saw myself in the round mirror hanging on the back of her door, and in the reflection, she pulled off those little ankle socks people seem to like and sits on the bed.

And she asked me, "What do you think?"

And I have no idea what she means, there is so much to choose from. So, I ask, "About what just happened?"

That's the first time I notice the golden strands are back, just a couple, drifting in the air off the back of her head. I check hands and mirror. No strands for me, even though they were there inside the TV.

"Did we just kill your parents?" I ask.

[Natalie Lavigne] [secret diary]

Millie, my mystery,

Are you perhaps the same, for lack of a better word, "person" as my parents? A collective? Perhaps you are another everyone?

I can see the myriad faces in the one face when I picture that "requisitioning." It always made sense that we had a part of us dedicated to determination and execution. That force that might act on the self to drive the self in all things. To fill out the tapestry.

And now for the first time, I can see the cruelty of it. It's cruelty I welcome, but sure. I am squishy. I can be hardened into a driven instrument. But for what? The plan laid out for me in that expanse. All the great and sprawling things I see I must accomplish to be the person I will be, that I drew out when I was a single golden thread?

That is a sound tapestry, still, and forever.

But I like cooking reality show binges! I like sitting under a tree and musing about the punchline of the delightful school comic strip Normal's Family. I like the limitations of kissing. I like trying to learn German with no stakes attached. Freut mich, tapestry!

Perhaps less is more.

I am grateful this is private, as my attempts to define in human terms what this all is seem utterly inadequate.

The Invitation

[Cole Abrams]

We bid adieu at the front door with a hug and when she goes back inside, the lights in the living room stay on.

I think... I don't know what to think anymore. She's all alone in there, but she's not. I don't know what I'd do without the sisters and mom. Even Harry.

Especially Harry. That guy just showed up outta nowhere and said yes to all of us. Just a yes person.

Nat is insufferable, confounding. But I never considered that maybe she was just unknowable. Or is that right? It's not that she's unknowable. It's that she wants to be something the opposite of what you are. But you're fun and connected and honest and...

And... I don't know. What's the thing when there's a person who is difficult and also you feel bad for them? Or no, it's not pity. I guess I just didn't appreciate what I had.

I don't know I don't know I don't know.

I feel lighter.

[Natalie Lavigne]

Sir,

Thank you for a lovely evening, complete with hoped for surprise and adventure.

Chuck Quimby's new comic strip is really lovely, tell her she's a triumph.

[Cole Abrams]

Thanks for inviting me over. I had a nice time too.

[Natalie Lavigne] [secret diary]

Millie,

Tell them not to come back. I will finish this study abroad on my own.

Please, leave the concert harp though. It vibrates pleasantly.

[Adult Lyle]

Hey, it's me. Old Man Lyle, of Bandido Cafe fame!

(Not old. Again, just forty-two. That was a joke.)

I came into the cafe today and the place was devoid of furniture and the espresso bar was gone. The couch had reverted back to its original size—a pocketable figurine roughly three inches long—and revealed quite a bit of dust on the floor where I haven't maybe been sweeping as well as I could. There was a whole croissant there! Yikes.

Ladies and germs and enbies, I regret to say that this means that it is time for Shadow Joe and me to move on and the Bandido Cafe to close.

This isn't a forever goodbye, but it is goodbye for now.

I have closed up shop tons of times at tons of jobs in my life, but never before have I felt so wistful about it. You kids have inspired me and surprised me. Your stories have been fun and funny and legitimately terrifying. I'll miss you all. Even you, JR.

Life is an unpredictable thing, but the one constant is that everything changes.

Ciao!

Oh, and Shadow Joe says, "11y01010 00xn1010 1010yy10 101n0101 x0010111 11010y01."

LOL, good one, my dude.

[Alexa Garcia]

I know what house I want to live in. This is a new development on account of a school years' worth of walking to PS13.

It's the one on Kent way up on the hill. The one with green sides and white windows and the tiny narrow driveway that was like made for a Model T or something. Every time I walk by it I look up and I just feel at peace, you know?

I don't know. I won't be a homeowner for a long time. Or ever. Maybe I should wait on picking out my future home. What if it gets swallowed whole in an earthquake?

Maybe if things go south again in adulthood, I can hide out up there, apart from the world, and the little kids (I'll be an old spinster then) will look up like I am and say, "What a cute little house, I'd like to live there some day."

And I'll look down and yell, "NO! It's mine! Get off my property!"

Haha.

I should make that into a poem.

Hmm. Haven't had that urge in a while.

[GOMEZ]

The four-winged bird showed up and knocked on my window and told me to "have a great instance of summer."

Thank you, bird. I think I might.

I have decided to learn how to swim! I will take a class at the community center.

Ebit has offered to be my official tango partner for the big Santa Barbara International Tango Bracket in July. Now that I am curse-free, I can have a steady dance partner without risking their life.

Also, there's a camp where you stay in a cliff face in Grand Canyon National Park and spend the days making pots like Native Americans did and at night we use our powers to remove information about Earth and humans from radio broadcasts in deep space.

The bird technically told me to take the pottery/earth defense camp, everything else was my idea.

[Phoebe Case]

It's hard to believe the year has gone so fast. We've had a blast, haven't we? There was drama, lots of romance and stuff, a big super fun dance. I even finally got to explain my secret to Gomez that I'm a twenty-six-year-old journalist.

He played it off and said he knew that already. Smooth, kid!

You may have noticed I sort of vanished there. I pitched my book to a certain magazine-slash-publishing house, about what really goes on in high schools in Los Angeles. And they bit! They said not to hold back, and I definitely have not. Want to do all y'all justice, y'know?

Kyle, Lance, Teemo, others from the bleachers (i.e., the girls): I promise to be fair but real.

It's been tough these last few weeks. A real grind. I keep sending my pages, but the editor is a real stickler. The most stickler-y editor I think I've ever seen. Lots of "what are you talking about, Phoebe? High schools don't have contraband magic artifacts." "What are you talking about, Phoebe? Students cannot fly." "What are you talking about, Phoebe? School lunches are not that exciting."

Au contraire, cute prickly editor man! You need to open your mind.

The endless struggle of a journalist. That's the path I've chosen, and I walk it gladly.

Who's doing summer school? See you there!

[DOCTOR M]

Daily step count: 15,035

Grace alerted me to an alteration in a student file.

These happen a couple of times a year when the timeline corrects. Maybe someone doesn't want a bridge to explode, or a particularly powerful extradimensional senior finally gets their act together and turns in years-old assignments at their past due date.

Educational structure can be motivating!

This was a weird one, though, as it concerned two adjacent files that changed at the same time. I eventually remembered. This was the result of my error at the start of the school year. I'd told the wrong student they would fight an ancient evil and lo (and behold!), she somehow made it happen, anyway. She worked for an evil tech conglomerate, made a hyper-powerful subtractive copy of themselves, and then traveled back in time and found her copy pre-rampage and merged with it, and caused (delightfully) a much much less destructive outcome than the original timeline gave us.

I'd say I'm chuffed, and I am. Mistakes rarely work out this well. But what of G. Alex, the original student destined to stop this specific Titan? I can't say offhand that I remember them. I am embarrassed. Their file has removed all references to fighting Lurkett in the change, leaving a fairly unremarkable student transcript.

Also, Alex is weirdly terrible at math in almost all its forms. He was like that before, right?

When a destined hero as possibility isn't given their moment, what happens then?

[Alex Ganz]

This is so weird. For months now this little wrinkly lady guy has been finding me on the street and pointing and yelling, "You are our only hope against Lurkett!" I got used to it; Nancy and I think it's funny now.

Congratulate me for using a semicolon!

She started to pretend the little crone was pointing at her too but saying things like, "The lady says I have to audition for one-act play again." Haha!

I'm not gonna lie. The promise of a big heroic fight made my anti-magic jujitsu classes and psychic burst training a little bit easier. I can fight like four people at once now, on account of all the extra fight practice.

Anyway, I just saw that wrinkly lady in front of the empty husk of Bandido's and she looked at me, pointed, inhaled to yell, and it was like someone was talking to her in an earbud because she just put her pointer finger away and shuffled off.

Alright, cool. The dude abides.

[Mikey12]

Hey I'm not dead! Just caught a blast of sad psychic juice from Alexa's carbon back at Vulcan and I guess that's what I needed to shake loose from permanent werewolf mode. So now I'm just li'l Mikey again.

I might have overreacted earlier. I was shocked at what it was like to be normal sized again. But there are definite benefits:

I can go to the movies, and no one screams and runs!

I can go to the mall, and no one screams and runs!

I can walk through doorways without the sideways shimmy and without taking my backpack off!

Clothes have some perks. Mostly pockets.

It's strange to scroll back through the posts on here and see what I was like way back at the start of the year. I was obsessed with conspiracies. I mean I still am. I've just grown and gotten wiser. And taller by a couple of inches.

I won't rule out another go at a conspiracy club. Just with a different name because The Question Society is radioactive after aaaall that. Hmm. Maybe Damien should be in charge. I read somewhere that if you force someone to be a leader when they don't want to be, they can't screw it up.

Late Bright Light Nights

[Seluvion]

I am nine thousand years young, and I still get picked on sometimes. Especially in physical education courses. Seluvion abides because this year I will finally graduate.

What lies beyond the event horizon that is high school graduation?

Is it as when a star is born in a burst of cosmic energy?

[Hep Marlo]

Hiiii, fellow seniors! We've made it to the end of our time here and let me be the first to say, good riddance! I have personally nearly exploded/died/disintegrated a half dozen times at Paranormal School 13. From 1) Fenix Ash, 2) 4D Hypercube Infestation (2019), 3) the Valentine's Day incident 4) The Blade Dancefall 5) 4D Hypercube Infestation (2021) and 6) The Skullhunters Maw attack last October.

As part of the graduation committee, we have been working all semester to ensure no shenanigans on our big day. We're going to have a SAFE, CRISIS-FREE graduation and escape back into the normal world and not look back. Some of you want to have supernatural adventure jobs and I think you are real crazy.

Late Bright Light Nights

Dentists unite! Who is with me?

[JR Benton]

If Camila weren't contained in the Maw I know she'd want me to be at graduation, to represent her and her grand accomplishments! Even though I guess she isn't technically graduating, and even if she weren't trapped in the Maw,
    Note to self: Start a band called Trapped In the Maw
    Or maybe just "In the Maw." Hmm.
    I should start with the T-shirts.

[Cole Abrams]

I can't believe I have to take time away from classes and SFS to do this dumb recital. Today they made us gather at the soccer field, then we have to sit there while Doctor M gives a little speech I guess he gives every year. ("We finally made it!" etc.) Then they make us line up in a bunch of rows like we will when we graduate and Ami Aawut gets to actually walk as an example (chosen first again, huh?). And by the time we're done, the final bell goes off and it's the mass exodus to the parking lot and busses.

[Rodney Gemini (Moon Facet)]

Cole why are you now being so salty, you are so chill on average.

[Rodney Gemini (Sun Facet)]

Let Cole be how he is, reflection. We are at a crossroads.

[JR Benton]

Uh, does anyone know how to get t-shirts made? Do you just… search for it on the internet?

[Cole Abrams]

You know what I think it is? I'm not ready to graduate.

Or maybe I don't want this part of things to end. It's not even that high school has been universally fun. If anything, it's frequently frustrating. And I'm not just talking about the weird stuff.

There's going to be a big noise and we'll throw our hats in the air (and they'll hang there indefinitely, probably, thank you fellow psychics). And then that's it and we all walk alone in separate directions into the afternoon. And in future decades, this will all seem more and more alien, but I'll still have dreams about being late to school and of my wrist beeping for an emergency periodically.

I don't think I had a chance to figure it out, brother. Y'know?

I was so busy being alarmed and combative and unsure, now it's all over. What have I actually done?

[JR Benton]

Can someone let me use your phone to look up how to make t-shirts?

[Seluvion]

It is done.

I am free. A kaleidoscope of possibility awaits. When I look back in nine thousand years, will it feel familiar, this place? This time?

I am Seluvion, a thing sculpted of stardust in forever motion across the black of space. And now, a graduate (with honors) of the Paranormal School System.

[Hep Marlo]

Thank you all for a fun, painless graduation!

[Cole Abrams]

In the end, they called up the person before me. They called me. They called the person after. I shook Doctor M's hand and the sisters yelled, "Cole has a baby face!" and Doctor M gave me a warm smile and said thank you.

Natalie came, too. She sat with that little wolf freshman (who is now a little guy again) and she gave me a big hug. Alexa shook my hand proper-like. And I said thanks.

And that was that. The family went to go get sushi after. Harry and Mom said they were proud of me, which is weird because... what was I gonna do? Not graduate? I guess not everyone does. Never seemed like a choice to me. So, I said thank you.

And I'm laying here staring at the ceiling in my room.

[Mayumi Ikazaki]

Freedom!
  I am
  outta
  here
  .

One of Grendma's ghosts promised to give me a secret, dangerous tour of Paris.

I'm sure spending exactly one semester at a high school will mean some therapy down the road, but I had fun.

I think it would be wrong to keep the hall pass that makes coyotes appear, but I will probably do it anyway. If only hall passes could talk. What's your story, old worn laminated hall pass tied to a ruler?

[JR Benton]

Bad news, bad news, bad news time, fam.

Bad news: T-shirt didn't get made (too many questions from the T-shirt bros)

Bad news: Missed graduation. Camila, please forgive me.

Bad news: IN THE MAW (the band) is over. This industry is raw.

Who is down for a beach bonfire?

Late Bright Light Nights

[Alexa Garcia]

It's getting really warm, and the sun is starting to set way later. I just got back from the pool. I didn't used to like swimming laps but now I sort of like it. Something sucks about the rhythm of it, and my arms and legs burn. I can't get air except every few strokes, but I feel like panicking less, and I feel the water rushing by and it's really relaxing, like gliding on air.

I should really ask Oliver how flying actually feels before I go and make up things about flying.

Bianca called and—

Oh, right. We're friends again. We never actually stopped being friends, I guess. After our fight I may have started avoiding her, and I didn't even realize. A couple of days ago at the cafe I saw her and managed to stay for a conversation where I was honest about how I've felt, and she called me out on it. How I acted, I mean.

I apologized. I don't think I would have been okay with the conversation before the showdown at the house. There were lots of feels coming up. I felt so relieved and also stupid but also... I dunno... more myself.

Okay, back to what I was saying. Bianca called and there's a big to-do at her house tonight—a summer vacation starting party. And in Bianca fashion, it's got refreshments but also a bunch of people volunteering to do music and standup comedy and stuff. And I have this little poem I've been working on, and I may have been talked into reading it by a certain very beautiful Danish girl with short hair and dimples. It's sort of a sequel to the one I performed last time. Or at least, it's got the blue cat in it again.

And I can't promise anything, but if the blue cat wanders into my path on my way to the performance... well, wouldn't that be crazy?

Second craziest thing I've seen all year.

Hmm. Maybe third.

XOXO

Paranormal School 13

Paranormal School System

- PS1 - ████████████████
- ~~PS2 - Depths of Veromang~~
- PS3 - Edinburgh, Scotland, UK
- PS4 - Rome, Italy
- PS5 - ████████████████
- PS6 - Toronto, ON, Canada
- PS7 - Asmara, Eritrea
- PS8 - Buenos Aires, Argentina
- PS9 - Kyoto, Japan
- PS10 - Hong Kong SAR
- PS11 - Perth, Australia
- ~~PS12 - Albany, NY, USA~~
- PS13 - Los Angeles, CA, USA
- PS14 - Mexico City, Mexico
- PS15 - Seoul, South Korea
- PS16 - ████████████████
- PS17 - ████████████████
- PS18 - Siberia, Russian Federation
- PS19 - Indian Ocean
- PS20 - TBD

Acknowledgments

Thanks to my fellow alums and the teachers from *my* time at a weird supernatural school, *Psychic High School.*

Thanks to Pamie, who gave this book its name in a moment so fast, it seems like a flex.

Thanks to my sister, who remains my first and biggest fan.

And a big, huge thank you to *you*, just for being you.

About the Author

Westin Lee does not exist.

He is the author of *Paranormal School 13, Tellermoon and Wicked City*. He writes science-fiction and fantasy in book form and movie form and TV and video game form. His webzone is westinlee.com.

He used to not exist in the suburbs of Houston under the wet, burning sky. Wanderlust hurtled him from city to city and medium to medium, from Berlin to Los Angeles, to webcomics and live comedy and film.

At last, he is home.

www.ingramcontent.com/pod-product-compliance
Ingram Content Group UK Ltd.
Pitfield, Milton Keynes, MK11 3LW, UK
UKHW061221180426
11946UKWH00020B/167/J